THE BRIDEGROOM

By

Margaret Brazear

A CHARLOTTE CHASE MYSTERY

Copyright © Margaret Brazear 2023

All rights reserved

CHAPTER ONE

The journey to Cornwall didn't take as long as Charlotte expected. She stopped a few times for the dogs to have a drink and a wee, but the traffic hadn't been nearly as bad as it was the last time she was here. Of course that had been in the summer months, when the roads were clogged up with holiday makers. Now it was autumn and there was a chill in the air. The sleepy little Cornish town was now almost exclusively occupied by locals, struggling along on what they had made from the tourists during the summer.

It was Charlotte's favourite time here and had been Aunt Florrie's, quiet except for the crashing waves hitting the beach from the Atlantic Ocean. This was to be the first day of the rest of her life and she felt sure she was going to love it!

It had just got too much in London, with Peter thinking he could still tell her how she should live, still trying to turn her into something she was not. Her talent embarrassed him; that was the long and the short of it and it was not as though she hadn't told him before they married. It had taken a long time for her to realise that he simply hadn't believed her, though why he imagined she would make up a story like that she could never fathom.

So after two years of his scoffing at the clients who came to her, of never wanting to know about her gift, of him being in denial, she had given up. Two things happened to push her into her final decision; firstly, he had a company dinner and dance which he didn't tell her about. He pretended it was a work conference that kept him away overnight and she had to find out purely by coincidence when one of his colleagues asked a friend of Charlotte's to the function.

His excuse was he didn't want her suddenly telling people their future or seeing ghosts everywhere and showing him up. As if she didn't know when to keep her mouth shut. His real motive was so he could sneak into the room of a woman he worked with, something he didn't expect to get back to Charlotte.

She was already considering her options when she'd been offered a television contract. She hadn't really wanted to take it; she'd always preferred to keep things private as much as possible, but she thought it would serve Peter right if her face appeared on millions of television screens. He would have a hard time pretending his wife was no different from theirs after that, wouldn't he?

It was a pity; she had never believed in divorce and still didn't, not really, but there was no other way. He had friends close by, he said, and he didn't want them knowing about his wife and her strange ideas. What would they think? She could no longer struggle to pretend.

That was a year ago and she hoped he might move away but his work was close by and his friends, the ones who would think his wife some sort of loony tunes and she could never afford to move. Until the house was sold, they were both stuck.

She charged nothing for her services, only took donations and although they were often generous, she didn't make much more than the cost of keeping her beautiful dogs.

When Aunt Florrie died and left her house in Cornwall to Charlotte, no one could have been more surprised. Florrie had never married and had no children, but Charlotte didn't expect her to leave the house to her. There was a few thousand pounds as well, which would come in handy.

This house went back to the Tudor dynasty, Elizabeth I to be precise and had been built in the shape of an E in her honour, like a lot of the grand houses built during her reign. In the distance, at the end of what was now the garden, were the ruins of the castle after which the house had been named.

It had originally been one of William the Conqueror's castles, put here to guard the coast from invading fleets and pirates, but it had been ravaged by the salt sea waves crashing against the walls in bad weather and it had been

It was the ones who wanted something who caused Charlotte so much aggravation, who caused Peter to decide she would have to pretend she didn't see them. She was coming up to thirty on her next birthday and she felt she had wasted five years of her life on him. This was her new start, her second chance; God bless Aunt Florrie!

She steered the vehicle around the curving driveway, bumped over a few cracks in the tarmac and pulled to a stop outside the front porch with its twin pillars either side of the carved oak door.

Charlotte jumped down and opened the sliding doors of the massive people carrier to release the two Newfoundland dogs who accompanied her everywhere. They both leapt out and headed straight for the nearest trees and walls to relieve themselves after the long journey, then returned to Charlotte to sit and stare at her in anticipation, no doubt wondering where they were and what was going to happen next.

Water, that's what. They needed water before anything else and she reached inside the vehicle to pull out her handbag and find the keys, a thick bunch of them given to her that morning by Aunt Florrie's solicitor. She also collected the dogs' water bowls and the milk and tea she had bought in the supermarket on the way. It seemed unlikely there would be anywhere in this remote part of the world where she could buy actual loose tea leaves and not those awful tea bags.

Inside she headed straight for the kitchen at the back of the house, tried the tap to discover which one was cold since the coloured bands had long since worn away, then filled the bowls with water and set them on the black tiled floor for the dogs.

She straightened up to see that, unusually, they were not following her but had stopped in the wide hallway. She went out, saw that both dogs were staring up the staircase to the half landing and knew that once again, they had seen something or someone who shouldn't be there. She sighed heavily.

"Couldn't you at least have waited until I got the kettle on?" Charlotte said to the phantom on the stairs.

She wouldn't look closely at it, not yet. She knew it was a woman but that was all she wanted to know right now. It would still be there when she had made a pot of tea and put her feet up for five minutes. She called the dogs to the kitchen for their water, where she filled and plugged in the electric kettle, thankful that no one had thought to turn off the supply and she was spared the need to rummage about in cupboards for the mains switch.

Forgetting their interest in the phantom on the stairs, the dogs were now slurping away at the deemed too expensive to repair. It had been allowed to decay and fall apart but there was still a spirit presence there, the castellan and his family.

They were content there and Charlotte saw no reason to disturb them. She had seen them first when she was just a child, when she'd come here on holiday with her mother and had visited the ruined castle. The family were carrying on as though she wasn't there, walking about, cooking their meals and eating them, sharpening their spears and polishing their shields.

Even as a child, Charlotte was enthralled by their beautiful clothes, their fancy tunics and embroidered kirtles of the woman and her daughters. Even then, she accepted that they were a family in spirit, no longer of this world.

It was quite fascinating to see them, to see the way they lived, the castellan and his wife and three children, still ensuring that the shores of England were safe.

Charlotte had never told anyone about it.

She didn't want a hoard of tourists coming here trying to see the ghosts themselves and she didn't want some busy body thinking they weren't at rest and wanting to help them cross over. They seemed very happy to Charlotte.

They could simply be shadows of their living selves, a sort of after impression as had been seen many times, like the Roman soldiers in York who marched some two feet below the ground and never saw the people in modern dress who watched them.

A large part of Castle House was in disrepair and Charlotte hoped it didn't cost too much to renovate and modernise. She still had a lot left from the television show and she could always renew that contract, as the production company wanted, if necessary.

There were some of the original Elizabethan fittings still in the house, which were well worth preserving. If things got dire, she might even be able to open it out to the public. That was something she had discussed often with Aunt Florrie, but she always resisted the idea and Charlotte agreed with her. Sometimes, though, she felt a little selfish that they were keeping this beautiful house all to themselves.

Interested people had always been able to make an appointment to come and look around, local historians and the like and Aunt Florrie had once allowed the local history society to hold a meeting here. That had gone down very well with the locals; they loved it.

Still, the thought of crowds of tourists traipsing all over Aunt Florrie's precious house was not one she wanted to contemplate. It would be a last resort; she would rather go back to the television.

She had to keep stopping as she drove through the winding streets of the town. There were a lot of people who seemed to be hanging about, waiting for something and Charlotte wondered if her arrival had clashed with a carnival or fete. But when she passed the church she saw it was a wedding that was holding her up and all these people were waiting to see the bride and bridesmaids.

Charlotte only hoped it turned out better for them than it had for her, but then perhaps he was more concerned with her happiness than his own image.

She pulled over to the side to make room for another car coming towards her, and while she waited, she glanced out of the window at the colourful costumes of the guests.

They looked expensive, every one of them. The six shivering bridesmaids who waited in the church porch were dressed in pure silk, each one a different colour, from pale lemon to coral to mint green. And each held a bouquet of white roses.

The cars parked along the narrow street were what car dealers would all 'prestige' – Rolls Royces, Aston Martins, BMWs, Mercedes and the like. Not a single old banger amongst them, not even something ordinary and a few years old.

Whoever this wedding was for, the cost of it would feed the starving of the world for years to come. Still, good luck to her; why not spend what you could afford? She did wonder what was taking so long though, but then the road

-7-

cleared and she edged forward slowly to safely negotiate the parked cars.

At the end of the street she came to a crossroads and shivered. Although it wasn't recorded anywhere, Charlotte knew from experience that a suicide victim was buried at this crossroads, had been buried here at about the same time as Castle House was built. She'd always wanted to find out more about her, but had never stayed long enough. Now perhaps she would have time to discover something of the woman's history.

She slowed the enormous people carrier she drove as the road fell steeply towards the beach. It was a quiet beach, one the tourists mostly left alone because no car park had ever been provided there. Space was scarce and the land belonged to Aunt Florrie, belonged to Charlotte now. Florrie wouldn't sell any of it and neither would her niece.

People could walk down there if they wanted, there was nothing to stop them, but there would be no car park.

She turned the final bend and at last the enormous old house came into view. Charlotte slowed down to admire it. She had always loved this house, although it was full of ghosts. Still, they were mostly harmless, just souls who had lived here in the past, been happy here and didn't want to leave. Charlotte had no problem with them and neither had Aunt Florrie.

It was the ones who wanted something who caused Charlotte so much aggravation, who caused Peter to decide she would have to pretend she didn't see them. She was coming up to thirty on her next birthday and she felt she had wasted five years of her life on him. This was her new start, her second chance; God bless Aunt Florrie!

She steered the vehicle around the curving driveway, bumped over a few cracks in the tarmac and pulled to a stop outside the front porch with its twin pillars either side of the carved oak door.

Charlotte jumped down and opened the sliding doors of the massive people carrier to release the two Newfoundland dogs who accompanied her everywhere. They both leapt out and headed straight for the nearest trees and walls to relieve themselves after the long journey, then returned to Charlotte to sit and stare at her in anticipation, no doubt wondering where they were and what was going to happen next.

Water, that's what. They needed water before anything else and she reached inside the vehicle to pull out her handbag and find the keys, a thick bunch of them given to her that morning by Aunt Florrie's solicitor. She also collected the dogs' water bowls and the milk and tea she had bought in the supermarket on the way. It seemed unlikely there would be anywhere in this remote part of the world where she could buy actual loose tea leaves and not those awful tea bags.

Inside she headed straight for the kitchen at the back of the house, tried the tap to discover which one was cold since the coloured bands had long since worn away, then filled the bowls with water and set them on the black tiled floor for the dogs.

She straightened up to see that, unusually, they were not following her but had stopped in the wide hallway. She went out, saw that both dogs were staring up the staircase to the half landing and knew that once again, they had seen something or someone who shouldn't be there. She sighed heavily.

"Couldn't you at least have waited until I got the kettle on?" Charlotte said to the phantom on the stairs.

She wouldn't look closely at it, not yet. She knew it was a woman but that was all she wanted to know right now. It would still be there when she had made a pot of tea and put her feet up for five minutes. She called the dogs to the kitchen for their water, where she filled and plugged in the electric kettle, thankful that no one had thought to turn off the supply and she was spared the need to rummage about in cupboards for the mains switch.

Forgetting their interest in the phantom on the stairs, the dogs were now slurping away at the water, spilling it all over the floor. They raised their heads and ribbons of drool hung off their jaws. Charlotte got out of the way before they shook their heads, decorating the walls with little swirls which she would wipe away later, when she'd recovered from the journey.

Right now her back was stiff from sitting in one position for so long and she needed a couple of Nurofen and a hot drink. She found Aunt Florrie's teapot in the cupboard and rinsed it out. It would be a bit stale, as it was six months since Florrie passed and no one had been here since, except the gardener and the daily cleaner who were both still being paid out of the estate.

Even with the Will naming Charlotte as beneficiary, it had taken all this time for her to be given possession. It was something to do with it being a listed building.

She looked down just in time to see Fritz put his huge front paw in the water bowl and made a mental note to bring the bowl stands in next. One reason she always had their water up high was because they could never resist paddling in it.

She went outside to collect the sack of dog food and return to the kitchen with it, only to find the dogs back in the hallway and staring at the staircase again. She would worry about that later, when she had made herself a cup of tea and explored her new home, when she had pulled herself together and pushed Peter and his new love interest to the back of her mind.

Even after she appeared in her own TV show, he didn't want to admit that the marriage was over. Even when she challenged him about the woman he had been seeing behind her back he tried to talk his way out of it. How did he imagine he could hide anything from her?

He didn't seem to understand at all that he had driven her away with his insistence on trying to mould her into his own idea of what she should be, instead of accepting her for who she was.

They had to stay together in the house until it was sold. They divided it up and shared the kitchen and bathroom, but he continued to behave as though they were still together. Charlotte knew he had told none of his work colleagues about the separation, not even the woman he had found to replace her.

He assured Charlotte there was nothing going on, nothing real at any rate. It had been a whole year since the divorce so why he thought he had to pretend for Charlotte, she could not imagine.

He seemed to think they were still a couple, that she still cared what he did and who he did it with. She didn't.

"It's just sex," he told her. "She means nothing to me."

Why did people say that? Why did they imagine that made it any better, as though sex is something completely separate from love and loyalty? Not for Charlotte, that was for certain, and he should have known that.

Thank goodness Aunt Florrie had waited to breathe her last until the divorce was final and Charlotte knew she had made that last Will after she got her Decree Absolute. She didn't want any part of her estate to go to Peter.

When she told him she was moving to Cornwall, that Aunt Florrie had left Castle House to her, he actually thought he was entitled to a part of it. He thought she was inviting him to go with her. She would always remember his first reaction to the news. There were no words of condolence, despite knowing that Charlotte was more than fond of the old lady. His first thought had been the best way to liquidate the estate.

"That sort of place will fetch a fortune," he had said at once. "Some rich American will lap up the history and it's right on the coast. It would make a great hotel."

"I am not selling it," she answered.

She had packed everything she could into her vehicle and now all that remained was a small bag containing her immediate essentials. She had waited deliberately until he arrived home to tell him in person that he could have the house to himself until it sold, but he didn't seem to take the hint.

"What do you mean, you're not selling?" He said. "I tell you what, Charlotte, this is fate. It is like a gift. We have been looking for something to bring us together and this is it. We could turn it into a fancy hotel. With all that history, we will be sold out."

"We?"

"Well, yes, we. You can't do it on your own."

She sighed heavily, picked up the last of the bags and slung the handle over her shoulder.

"Peter, listen carefully. We are divorced. We are no longer a couple, no longer legally tied together and the only reason we still share this house is because we cannot afford to do otherwise until it sells. Now you can either buy me out of my half, or stay until it does sell, but the sooner you are out of my life for good, the better."

"Charlotte," he argued. "We can start again, give it another go. You loved me once and I still love you."

Yes, she had loved him once, although memories of that time, of those feelings, were blurred. She couldn't recall feeling anything for him but contempt. He was attractive to look at, with his blonde hair and piercing blue eyes, but since their marriage he had let himself go to some extent. She had definitely fancied him, but she couldn't drag up any memory of actually loving him.

At last she answered.

"No you don't and I don't think you ever did. Ever since we met you have tried to turn me into something else, some image of what you think I should be. I wish you luck in finding that woman, but if you are looking for her in me, you are looking in the wrong place."

"After everything I have put up with, you are not going to give me another chance?"

"What, precisely, do you think you have put up with?"

He gestured toward the two dogs who sat, patiently following the conversation as though they understood every word. Charlotte would say they did and she really believed that, but now was not the time to argue the point.

"Those two great, hairy, drooling beasts," Peter replied. "Do you know how many times I have found their hair all over my suit?"

"You should have been more careful. You know how much they moult."

"And what about the embarrassment of you being on television, like the boy in that film. 'I see dead people,' was what he said, wasn't it?"

Charlotte shook her head, feeling relieved now to be going. She used to love this man; now she hoped never to see him again.

She opened the front door and left the house, the dogs following, then slid open the side door and they both leapt inside, while she shut them securely in and climbed into the driver's seat.

"Charlotte," Peter called after her. "I haven't finished. We need to talk."

"Goodbye, Peter," she answered as she put

the gear lever into drive, released the brake and drove away.

She had her two beautiful baby bears, Fritz and Freya, her enormous, hairy canines who meant more to her than anything or anybody. They would settle into their new home and they would go for daily walks along the beach, they would play together in the massive waves and they would settle down to a future without him. Peter would have no part in her inheritance nor in her new life; serves him right.

***

Samantha was beginning to be familiar with this passing scenery.

This was the third time the limousine had driven passed the medieval church where hundreds of guests waited to see her walk down the aisle on the arm of her father.

She had argued with him constantly since the day she accepted Simon's proposal and he would be so very pleased to know it had all gone wrong.

Simon was a mechanic, very skilled and on his way up in his profession, even had his own little workshop, but Samantha would inherit her father's millions when he died. He had made those millions in trade, which left him still not quite in favour with the upper classes who looked down on such a thing.

It was strange that even after centuries of class distinction, earning an honest living was still not quite the thing. That fact still smarted with Samantha's father, who was in better financial condition than most of the nobility.

Since his daughter was born he had cherished a hope that she would marry into the English aristocracy, but the days of the million dollar princesses were long gone. They were the daughters of American millionaires who were bartered to earls and dukes and their heirs in order to restore their fortunes. Those girls were without exception American; the nobility couldn't possibly have an English commoner rescue them from penury.

Why was her mind wandering to such trivialities when she had far more important things to worry about? Like why her bridegroom had not yet arrived and what the hell had delayed him? A sudden sinking of her heart assured her that this was something to do with her father. He had been trying to break them up since they first met, had even tried to buy Simon off but he wouldn't take the money. Simon loved her; she was sure he loved her.

There had been a pre-nuptial agreement, what the Americans called a pre-nup. The old man had insisted on it or he would have given his fortune away to charity. That was all right, not something Samantha worried about.

The agreement was that should there be a

divorce, or even if he outlived her, Simon would not get a penny. She had no intention of ever parting with Simon anyway.

Fourth circuit. Samantha looked anxiously at the clock on the dashboard of the silver Rolls Royce which her father had bought specially to take her to the church. He couldn't hire a car like everybody else, could he? He had to show off by buying one. Her mind wandered again and for the first time she wondered what he would do with it after today. Keep it for show probably.

She fished her phone out from the side pocket of the door and dialled Simon's number, again. It went straight to voicemail, again.

Damn! Where was Simon?

***

It was growing dark before Samantha agreed to give up and have the chauffeur take her home. She'd cried herself to sleep that night and now she sat twisting her diamond engagement ring and staring out at the beautifully landscaped acres her father was so proud of. Behind her on the table were the wedding gifts, still wrapped, reminding her of the day her world fell apart.

There were also a pile of unopened greetings cards, about three hundred of them, that no one had felt like opening.

She'd insisted on being driven passed that church for another hour or more before she'd been persuaded to give up and be driven home, sobbing, her make up blurred and mascara blackening her cheeks as it blended with her tears.

She was inconsolable that day and the next. She'd rung Simon more times than she could count, until at last his voicemail told her it was full and could accept no more messages. That meant he hadn't opened the ones she'd already left and that meant he either didn't want to hear them or for some reason didn't have his phone with him.

She had phoned all the hospitals in the area and the police, but there was still no sign of Simon.

She tried to drive to his workshop, above which was the small studio flat where he lived. She wanted to see if he was there, perhaps ill or hurt and no one to know about it. But her father had taken the car keys and insisted on driving her there himself.

"You can't drive in this state," he had told her and for once she conceded he was right.

But Simon was not there, the flat was empty and his phone was lying on the small table beside his bed, the battery almost dead.

The visit had resulted in more tears and she wished her father would stop assuring her she was better off without him.

"Why should he leave me like that?" She demanded. "If he wanted the money, like you believe, why should he give up the chance of getting it?"

He hesitated for a moment before answering, then he put his arm around her soothingly.

"It was after the pre-nuptial agreement, when he realised he wouldn't get a penny. That's when I found his price, Samantha," he said.

"What?"

"A quarter of a million, in cash. I took it round there the day before the wedding, left it on the doorstep. I knew that if he was genuine he'd bring it straight back, but he didn't."

She pulled away, stared at him with horror in her eyes.

"So you knew he wouldn't turn up at the church, but still you let me go ahead with it?"

"I didn't know, Samantha. I hoped he might do the right thing."

"You are a bloody liar!" She screamed at him.

That was yesterday and now she sat miserably wondering how she could get in touch with Simon, find out what he really felt. Despite the missing money and her father's insistence that he had taken it, she still didn't believe it.

Her mind wandered back to the happy times they had shared, to the love she had felt from Simon. She still didn't believe he would take the money and run.

She went to the police station that morning,

reported him as missing, but she could see by the poorly concealed smirks they didn't believe her. And she wasn't a relative, Simon was an adult. They'd put him on the missing persons list but that was all they could do.

She'd begged her father to report it as well, knowing his name carried a lot of influence in the area and he said he had done so, but she didn't really believe him. She was just wondering if she should hire a private investigator herself to find Simon; that seemed to be the only thing she could do now.

She heard the door open but made no move to get up or even turn her head. It would be her mother again, come to ask her once again what she was planning to do with the unopened gifts. Since they had come from her father's friends, she had no doubt they were expensive. They would all have tried their best to compete with each other, try to be the one whose gift cost the most. That was what you got when you were a multi-millionaire – sycophants.

The gifts should be returned, but Samantha still clung to the hope that Simon would get in touch and the wedding would go ahead. There had to be a good reason he had simply not turned up at the church, without a word. He would turn up, with a motive for his absence and the missing money which she would never have considered.

She'd phoned all the hospitals again, local as

well as farther afield, and she had driven every road within a fifty mile radius, looking for his car. She had stopped on every coast road and looked down the cliffs, hoping to see his car there while hoping not to see it at the same time. But what else would have caused him to leave her like that, without a word? Nothing but an accident and perhaps he had lost his memory? But all the hospitals had said the same thing, that they had not had an accident that day or the day before. She was clutching at straws now and she knew it.

"Samantha, dear," her mother said. "We must decide what to do with the gifts. People will start to wonder if you don't return them soon."

"If they want them back they should say so."

"Of course they won't do that. It would be the height of ill manners."

"I thought my not returning the gifts was the height of ill manners."

"Don't be awkward, darling. You know what I mean."

She turned as the door opened again, this time admitting her father. Samantha could not help but notice that while her mother looked distressed, knowing as she did how people would be gossiping, her father had a little satisfied gleam in his eye.

"Right, this afternoon I shall arrange to have all these presents returned to the people who so generously gave them. It has to be done. We need to draw a line under this business and move on, find you a decent man to marry."

"You mean a rich one," Samantha replied. "Or preferably one with a title. Why have you done nothing about finding Simon?"

She had asked him yesterday to hire private investigators to look for Simon. He had the money to employ the very best and she saw no reason why he hadn't done so.

"What is there to do?" he answered. "He realised he was doing a bad thing, took the money and ran."

Samantha felt her cheeks beginning to burn with anger. Ever since she had become engaged to Simon, her father had been upping the bribes he offered him to go away.

Even the pre-nuptial agreement hadn't frightened him off and her father couldn't stand to be wrong.

Samantha shook her head, feeling thoroughly disgusted with him.

"Why do you think every man is only after your money?" She demanded. "Could it not be possible that he actually loved me?"

"Of course, darling, but we needed to be sure, didn't we?"

"When I hear it from his own lips, I will believe it. Until then the wedding presents stay where they are and I don't want to hear another word about it."

She grabbed her handbag and strode from the

room, outside and to her Porsche. She needed to get away, needed to see friends who knew Simon, who knew he wouldn't desert her for any amount of money.

At this time of day she would find them in the Oceanside Café.

***

Charlotte had unpacked, fed the dogs and found the television set.

From the French windows in the sitting room she could see the garden with its now bare flower beds and beyond that, the castle ruins and the sea.

She had always loved this view. It reminded her of one of those old smuggler stories which were always set in Cornwall, and she was often surprised to see everyone in modern day clothing. There were some parts which never changed, where she expected to see women walking about in bonnets and long skirts.

She could hear the waves crashing against the rocks as the tide came in, a comforting sound which she loved. But she missed Aunt Florrie; it didn't seem right to be in this house without her, but there was no sign of her ghost anywhere. She had moved on, been content that Charlotte would have her property and she had no reason to stay.

Charlotte crossed the hall to get to the kitchen,

to pour another mug of tea from the pot before it got cold. She'd found Aunt Florrie's teapot, but hadn't been able to find her tea cosy.

The hall was about the size of the lounge in her old house in London and it was one of the smallest rooms in the house. The bare oak staircase was set in the centre, with heavily carved posts either side connecting to the bannister rails.

She didn't want to look up, but she knew she would have to. She sighed. She supposed she ought to deal with her unexpected and uninvited visitor who had followed her about ever since she first saw her standing on the half landing, with that familiar, appealing look in her eyes.

She got her tea and returned to the living room, only to see her standing beside the huge, stone fireplace, the dogs staring at her expectantly.

"Ok," she said. "Who are you and what do you want?"

The phantom opened her mouth but nothing came out. That usually meant they had only recently passed and hadn't yet got the hang of making their voice heard.

"You'll have to speak up," Charlotte said. "I don't do lip reading."

"Miranda," came a hoarse whisper.

The image was more solid now than when Charlotte had first seen it and she could see the gashes and bruises on the woman's face. Then the hand reached up and pulled the collar of her white blouse away from her neck, revealing angry bruises.

"You were strangled?" Charlotte asked. "And badly beaten by the looks of things."

The phantom nodded, reached out a hand to Charlotte which moved through her and made her shiver. She wished they wouldn't do that; it was a very disconcerting feeling.

"You poor thing. That is a shame," Charlotte said. "But I don't suppose you remember where it was? Or who it was?"

She had seen this before. They came to her, wanting to move on but too agitated to go and they never knew precisely what it was that had happened to them or what they wanted from Charlotte. She hoped this one didn't just want her to inform her family as that was where the trouble always started. People very often didn't believe that Charlotte had seen their dead relatives and started to accuse her of wanting to extort money from them, even though she never asked for anything.

"Miranda, you say," she said. "Well, you work on your memory and I'll talk to you tomorrow."

CHAPTER TWO

Samantha sat in her car trying to summon the courage to go inside the shore front café, where several of her friends were gathered at the window table. It was a big, circular building, mostly made of glass, and she could clearly see her two bridesmaids there.

Their talk seemed to be animated and Samantha could easily guess the topic of the conversation – her and her runaway bridegroom. Could there ever have been a better piece of gossip to hit this little seaside town? When was the last time a bride had been left standing at the altar, especially a bride as wealthy as her?

Well, she couldn't hide forever; she had to face her friends and neighbours, find out their views and put forward her own. It had been a couple of days but if there was one thing she knew about Simon, it was that he would not have just gone, just left her there like an idiot with everyone feeling sorry for her and never even bothering to phone.

Even if he had decided to take her father's money, which she didn't believe for one minute, he would at least have left a note.

No, something had happened to him, she was certain of that and she was just as certain that nobody would believe it. They would all think she was kidding herself, trying to save face. And in the meantime, no one was searching for Simon.

At last she summoned the courage to get out of the car and go to the café, join her friends and find out what the latest consensus was. They looked up as she opened the door, two of them, both bridesmaids at the wedding and both witnesses to her humiliation.

They stood, arms out to hold her as she reached the table.

"You poor, poor thing," Kim said.

"Have you heard anything from Simon?" This from Sophie.

"Come and sit down, tell us how you are."

Samantha sat, raised a hand to order a latte. It was her usual order so she needn't be explicit. The waiter knew what she always drank.

"How do you think I am," she answered angrily. "Simon has gone missing. Something must have happened to him and my father refuses to do anything to find him."

Her two friends exchanged glances.

"He'll turn up," Kim said. "Though what you'll say to him when he does I can't imagine. Leaving you like that with all those people watching. I hope you don't even think about taking him back after that."

Samantha collapsed back in her chair in an angry gesture.

"I might have known you wouldn't believe me either," she said. "I suppose you both think the same as my father, that he was only after my money. Well, I won't believe that until I hear him say it."

She wasn't going to tell them about the bribe her father had given him. That would give them more fuel for their conviction that he was a gold digger.

The waiter brought her drink and as he set it down on the table, she looked up to see a little, sympathetic smile on his lips that was easy to interpret. Even he felt pity for her.

Kim sat up straight in her chair, wanting to change the subject and longing to tell her friends her own small piece of news. Samantha's tragedy had to come first, but she would burst if she didn't tell them soon.

"All right," she said. "Guess what I heard?"

Samantha kept her eyes firmly on her phone, where she was texting Simon once again, even knowing he'd left his phone behind. Sophie forced some interest into her expression as she looked at her friend. She really wanted to ponder the missing bridegroom some more, but it seemed callous to harp on it.

"What?" She asked.

"Guess who's moved into Castle House?"

"That old place by the beach where Florrie Mason lived?"

Kim nodded vigorously but made no reply,

wanting to prolong the suspense for as long as possible.

"Well?" Sophie urged. "I thought the National Trust were going to buy it."

"First I heard of it," Kim answered.

These rumours seemed to start out of thin air. Just because the house was so old and a listed building, people made up their own minds what should happen.

Samantha showed no interest at all, still stared at her keypad, still deep in thought and hoping the phone would bleep with a reply from Simon.

"Charlotte Chase," Kim answered at last.

"Charlotte Chase the TV medium?" Finally, Samantha looked up at Kim and her eyes showed some animation.

"That's the one," Kim answered. "Apparently, she was Miss Mason's niece and her only relative, so naturally she's inherited everything. She moved in a couple of days ago."

"How do you know?"

"Our cleaner saw her arrive with two of the most enormous dogs you ever saw in your life. You know, she used to clean for Miss Mason and she went down there on the off chance, to see if anyone had taken it over yet."

"Will she be cleaning for the new owner then?" Sophie asked.

Kim shrugged.

"Not sure. She said she wasn't cleaning up

after those two hairy beasts, but I expect she'll change her mind if the money and the gossip's good."

Samantha got to her feet, pushed her chair back in the same motion and grabbed her bag.

"Where are you going?" Kim asked.

"I am going to introduce myself to our new neighbour. Perhaps she can tell me what has happened to Simon."

She ran out of the café and back to her car before they could stop her. Suddenly there was a chance and she was anxious to take it.

There had to be someone who could help her, someone who would take her seriously and not think of her as the poor, deluded girl who had been jilted at the altar.

She didn't believe her father's claim that Simon had taken his money. He had offered Simon money before, in ever increasing amounts, but he had never taken a penny. Father said that was because he wanted the lot and he would only get that by going through with the marriage.

That's when he had suggested the pre-nuptial agreement, expecting both Samantha and Simon to refuse to sign it.

But he was wrong; they had both been willing to sign it. They had gone further and agreed that should she die first, her fortune would go into a trust for any children they may have or, if no offspring were forthcoming, she named certain charities to which to entrust it.

She would have done anything to prove to her father that Simon loved her, not her wealth and she would not believe he had simply taken the money and gone.

Now she had sunk to a last resort, to consulting a medium of all things. She believed most of those people were charlatans, but she had watched Charlotte Chase's TV show and she was very convincing. She was still sceptical, but what had she got to lose?

The coast road was narrow and windy and Samantha was really a little scared of this car. It was her father who had insisted on buying it for her, when she really preferred something less powerful and she had always planned, when she married, to give this to Simon and get something a little more to her liking.

Her father had made his money through sheer hard work and guile, with little education and even less capital, and he always wanted to show off by buying expensive toys for his family, whether they wanted them or not.

Castle House was only about ten minutes from the main town. It was one of those typical Cornish places, big enough to be a small town but without the benefit of a town hall or its own mayor. There was a winding, cobbled road going down a steep hill to the beach on which no one but the disabled and residents were allowed to drive during tourist season.

Samantha lived in a big house just outside the town, another of Jason Montfield's acquisitions, bought specially to show his status. She didn't really blame him; after all he had come from working class people in east London, had always had to work to help support the family and to have made the millions he had was an achievement not to be downplayed. However, his insistence that every man Samantha was ever attracted to was only after her money was insulting. Why couldn't he see that?

She applied the brake changed into second gear as the road led steeply downhill and around a sharp bend to reveal the gates which had once been electric, but which Miss Mason had given up on years ago. Samantha wondered if they still worked but it was hardly important.

She drove between the massive gateposts and around the circular drive to the front door, where she stopped the car, switched off the engine and got out, mentally preparing herself for more scepticism when she explained her case.

She stood gazing at the house, looking for any sign of habitation and from deep within she heard the sound of a barking dog, an echoing, thunderous bark, obviously not from a small dog. Her friend had said the new owner had arrived with two enormous dogs, so it should have come as no surprise.

She almost turned away then, got back in her

car and left. She shouldn't have come. The poor woman had only just arrived and just because she had briefly hosted a television series did not give Samantha leave to disturb her. She was probably still mourning the loss of her aunt, as well as unpacking and finding her way about the enormous house.

That was what came of being brought up wealthy; you tended to think your money gave you the right to do precisely what you wanted. That is what her father believed; at least it seemed that way to Samantha, but she had a little more finesse.

He was brash and forthright, showed his working class East End roots every time he opened his mouth, and she loved him for it, but the schools to which he had sent her gave her something of a social advantage.

That was when the door opened and brought forth two massive dogs, one black and one brown and both looking like giant, animated teddy bears.

They ran towards her and she feared they might jump up and knock her over so she pushed herself back against the car in anticipation. But they stopped when they reached her and just sniffed at her hands, making sure they would recognise her again.

It was a good thing she had no fear of dogs, despite her father only ever keeping guard dogs who lived in kennels in the grounds.

"Hello," Charlotte said.

Samantha raised her eyes from the dogs who came up almost to her chest to see their owner standing on the porch, a curious look in her brown eyes, her short and wavy dark hair in disarray.

She made no excuses for the dogs' proximity to her visitor, gave no reassurance that they were harmless, which Samantha would have expected, especially given their size. But she supposed she was the intruder here, a total stranger arriving without invitation or notice on the doorstep of a television personality. Why should she give any such assurance?

Samantha put out a hand to the head of the black dog to stroke him, then she smiled, for the first time since the wedding that never was.

"What magnificent creatures," she said. "What are they?"

"They are Newfoundlands," Charlotte replied. She stepped forward and touched the head of the black one. "This is Fritz." She reached out her other hand to the brown dog. "This is Freya, his sister."

Still she didn't ask what her visitor wanted, which was odd. Samantha wondered if her gifts were as good as the television would have it and that perhaps she already knew.

"Forgive me," she said. "I am Samantha Montfield. I live close to the town and I heard that you had taken over the Castle House, that you were Miss Mason's niece."

"That's right."

"I came to welcome you as a neighbour," Samantha said quickly, suddenly afraid of disclosing her real reason for the visit. "That is, if you are planning to stay."

Charlotte smiled then, a warm smile but somewhat amused just the same. Samantha had grown accomplished at identifying sceptical smiles, not just over the past week but since she got engaged to Simon really. Nobody believed in him but her.

Charlotte stepped aside and gesture toward the door.

"Please, come inside. The place is thick with dust and cobwebs and all I've had time to do is unpack, but I expected that. Aunt Florrie couldn't do a lot and the cleaner she had was pretty useless."

Samantha caught her breath. Of course, she knew the woman; she cleaned for all the well-off families in and around the town.

"Why do you say that?" She asked.

"She didn't touch the upstairs," Charlotte replied. "Aunt Florrie moved downstairs a few years ago because of her arthritis so there was no one to oversee the woman. She took advantage."

"She cleans for us," Samantha said.

She expected Charlotte to be embarrassed, to wish she hadn't spoken her thoughts on the subject.

"Really?" Charlotte answered. "Perhaps you should check the places that are not much used."

Just as with the lack of apology for the dogs, Samantha was again surprised. Charlotte didn't look at all put out that her guest knew the subject of the conversation, nor did it seem to have occurred to her that she could be someone close. She didn't seem to care a lot.

She followed Charlotte inside to where the dogs had taken up a position at the bottom of the old oak staircase, staring up, focussed on something halfway up, something Samantha couldn't see. She shivered, felt goose bumps erupting over her skin. There was something eerie about this house, a house Samantha had always wanted to get inside and explore.

Charlotte looked up and smiled, but didn't call the dogs away. She led the way into the kitchen and plugged in the kettle.

"Tea?" She asked.

"Coffee, please."

"Sorry, I don't drink the stuff. I usually keep a jar for guests but I haven't had time to go shopping yet."

She turned back to the big, country kitchen table and gestured to a chair, which Samantha pulled out and sat on.

"Now, my dear," she said. "Perhaps you'd like to tell me the real reason for your visit and if it has anything at all to do with the phantom who has taken up residence on my staircase."

CHAPTER THREE

Her forthright question took Samantha by surprise and her mention of a phantom gave her the shivers. Why, she could not have said. After all, the woman was a medium, supposedly in contact with the dead, but she didn't expect her to talk about a spirit the same way she would about a breathing, living being.

What did she expect? A round table, gold gossamer or silk table cloth, lots of people sitting around it holding hands, knocks and bumps and 'is anybody there'? Perhaps a crystal ball and a pack of tarot cards. Probably.

Why didn't the woman know already why Samantha had come? If she was any good, surely she would know, wouldn't she?

"Don't you know?" Samantha challenged her.

Charlotte sat at the table and sighed.

"Ah," she said. "It's going to be one of those conversations is it?" She closed her eyes, emphasising the motion, then reached out and took Samantha's hand. "You have had a recent heartbreak over a man. I feel there have been a lot of arguments over this man. You are wealthy; he is not. That has probably upset your father who thinks he is only after your money, money he made through sheer hard graft and a nose for an opportunity. Am I right so far?"

Samantha's eyes widened. How did this stranger know so much about her, about Simon and her father? It seemed she was just as clever as everyone said she was.

"How do you know all that?" She said.

Charlotte sighed again. Everyone asked, always. They knew she was psychic; that was why they came, but still they were surprised to be given the simplest and most obvious information.

"Do you really want to know?" Charlotte replied. "Or would you rather keep your illusions?"

"You know things about me, yet we have never met before. Do you really see those things?"

Charlotte smiled, shook her head slowly.

"Your car is what? Fifty thousand pounds' worth? Yet your ring, while not cheap, is not top of the range. That is how I know that you are wealthy but your fiancé is not. It follows, therefore, that your father would not be happy about the marriage and might suspect the young man of being a gold digger. I imagine he would have tried many times to talk you out of it, might even have tried to buy him off." She paused to gage her guest's reaction.

"That would be my guess. Your eyes are puffy, telling me you have cried a lot recently and your finger beneath the ring is red and sore, which tells me you have been twisting it constantly for at least a day or two. That, in turn, tells me the cause of your distress is the fiancé."

"Oh," Samantha said, her heart sinking. She did not expect to be so easily duped. "That doesn't explain how you know about my father, how he made his money."

Charlotte reached out to a pile of post and junk mail which she had dumped on the table when she arrived after skimming through it. She tossed the parish magazine toward her guest.

"There is an article in here about him. Apparently he has been generous enough to pay for a new church roof. There is a nice family group picture to go along with the write up. You take a lovely photo."

Samantha blushed and looked down at her hands again. She felt embarrassed now, having been fooled by this woman. She wondered how many other people had fallen for a medium who was really nothing but exceptionally observant.

"Do you have some perceptive way of telling me the name of my fiancé?" Samantha demanded.

Charlotte shook her head.

"No. I only know his name begins with an S." She pointed to Samantha's bracelet from which hung a charm with two Ss entwined. "Something else I don't know; who is Miranda?"

Samantha felt her heart leap. There could be no trick to this, no extra perceptive observance. She looked down at herself, just to be sure that she had nothing that would indicate how the name could be of any significance. She knew, of course, there was nothing.

"How do you know about her?"

"Ah, well, that is another matter. You recall I mentioned the phantom on my staircase?"

Samantha spun around in her seat. She could see through the kitchen door to the hallway, to where the two dogs were still staring, their gazes fixed, towards the stairs.

"She is Simon's ex-girlfriend," Samantha answered, turning back. "But you can't have seen her ghost. She is not dead."

"Tell that to the baby bears," Charlotte said, gesturing to the dogs in the hallway. "She is there all right, no doubt about that, and she started to point and get quite agitated when you walked in. She can't say a lot yet, but she managed to tell me her name."

"Mandy," Samantha replied. "She was always called Mandy. Simon went out with her for about six months and she got quite obsessed, started booking venues for their wedding and everything. He found her quite creepy and he had broken it off when he met me."

"And how did that come about?"

"You mean how did a millionaire's daughter meet and fall for a mechanic?"

"Ah, a mechanic. I imagine he repaired your car." Charlotte looked over her shoulder to the shining silver Porsche on the driveway. "But not that car. That car's brand new."

"I think that's why my father bought it," Samantha replied. "Because he knew Simon would never be able to repair it. It's got computerised and micro chipped everything. He certainly didn't buy it for me; I hate the thing. It goes too fast, it is too low down and there's no room to give anyone a lift."

"So, what's been happening?" Charlotte asked. "Why have to come to see me?"

"I thought you might have heard. I'm sure the whole village is talking about it, if not the whole of Cornwall."

"Well, I only just got here. I had no idea Aunt Florrie was going to leave this place to me, but I'm very glad she did. I do feel that you have been frustrated, that your efforts to convince everyone of something have met with scepticism."

"You're right. Our wedding day was last Saturday, but Simon didn't turn up. He left me, riding around and around the church in a brand new Rolls Royce like an idiot. But no one has seen him since and I can't get any reply from his number. I went to his flat and his phone was there; he hadn't taken it with him, wherever he went. He wouldn't have done that to me; I know he wouldn't but can I get anyone to believe me? No. My friends, my family, even the police all think I am trying to save face."

So that was the wedding that had held Charlotte

up on her way here.

"So Simon has gone missing and you are worried about him?"

Samantha nodded feeling at last she had found someone who wouldn't dismiss her concerns as nothing more than an embarrassed, jilted girl trying to pretend it didn't happen that way.

She could tell by the compassion and concern in Charlotte's dark eyes that she believed her.

"You believe me, don't you?" Samantha said with a note of relief.

"I do. You knew Simon better than anyone, after all, but you will have to face the possibility that he was no more than a clever con artist, after your father's fortune. Some of those people are very convincing."

Samantha shook her head.

"No. He loves me; I know he does."

"Let's start with Miranda. There is a reason she is here and you tell me she is still in this world. I can tell you without doubt that she is not, she is in spirit and desperately trying to tell someone where to find her."

That was when the dogs came into the kitchen and started toward their huge water bowls, now set into the high stands so they could drink without bending down too far and without being tempted to paddle.

"She's gone," Charlotte said. "She was only waiting for us to recognise that her body was lying dead somewhere, but she'll be back."

"How do you know she's gone."

"The dogs have come in, stopped watching. They always watch the phantoms who come to visit. I don't know why, whether they want to be sure they don't intend any evil or what I don't know."

"I thought animals were frightened of ghosts."

"Not necessarily. They know a malevolent spirit when they see one and then they will run and hide somewhere, but any other sort they are just curious about."

Fritz, the big black dog, came to sit beside his mistress. She reached for a tissue from the box on the table to wipe away the strings of drool that hung either side of his mouth.

It was not a pleasant sight and Samantha hoped he didn't come near her still drooling. Her clothes were all very expensive and she was quite sure Charlotte would not help her if she insulted one of her precious dogs.

"They always do that when they've been drinking," Charlotte commented as she grabbed another tissue and called Freya to her side to wipe her mouth as well. She kissed the dog's head then turned back to Samantha.

"So, tell me about Miranda. She's been causing you grief, I expect."

"She wouldn't let go. She kept sending messages to Simon, flowers, kept following him everywhere. Wherever we went, she would appear. She wouldn't accept our engagement. She even tried to tell me that she and Simon had plotted together, that he would marry me for my money then get rid of me somehow so they could be together."

"You didn't believe her?"

"No, of course not. If that were true she'd have nothing to gain by telling me, would she? I half expected her to turn up at the wedding, just to cause trouble."

"Why do you think she didn't? Could it have been because she had passed over?"

"It wasn't a scenario I considered," Samantha said.

"Well, she is definitely in spirit now."

"And Simon?"

"I can't say," Charlotte said. "They only come to me when there is a problem. But he has gone missing and his ex-girlfriend, who was apparently stalking him, has passed over. That tells me, and should tell you, that he is not in a position to contact you."

Samantha twisted her ring once more then looked up at her hostess. She knew she had a pleading look in her eyes, knew she sounded desperate, but she had given up worrying about that.

"Will you help me, Miss Chase?" She asked.

"Only if you call me Charlotte. What have you done so far, to try to find him?"

"First I was angry, just waited for him to get in touch. So the answer is not much."

"Ok, the first thing we do is go to his home. Does he live alone?"

Samantha nodded.

"He's got a flat, just a studio flat over the garage where he works. But I've been there already. That's how I found his phone."

"Is it his own place, or does he work for someone?"

"It's his. He took out a thumping great bank loan to buy it and get it going. The previous owner just let it go to rack and ruin so he got it cheap."

"Well, that's where we start."

***

"Do you have a key?" Charlotte asked when they pulled up outside the garage where Simon worked and lived. It seemed to be an old, converted warehouse, with a big sign at the top of the double doors which read: Chandler's Motor Repairs.

"Yes," Samantha replied.

She pulled it out of her handbag and showed it to Charlotte. They had come in Charlotte's people carrier as she had refused to get into the Porsche, said it was too low down and there was no room for the dogs.

"I'm not leaving them," she said. "We've only

just got here and I won't leave them in a strange place."

So Samantha had sat in the front passenger seat with Freya peering out of the windscreen, her huge head close to Samantha's shoulder. Occasionally, she would turn and lick Charlotte's ear which seemed a bit dangerous to her passenger.

"I'm sure the experts would say they should be in cages in the car or those silly harnesses, but I think they are better off as they are. They don't like being restrained."

Outside the garage, which was locked up, they all got out of the vehicle and walked around to the back of the building where there was an iron fire escape leading up to the door to the flat. They started to climb, the dogs lay down on the ground beside the bottom step.

"They don't do stairs," Charlotte said.

At the top of the staircase, Samantha shoved the key into the lock and opened the door. There was post on the floor, just a couple of bills and a card from a friend of Simon's congratulating him.

When she'd been here before, Samantha's father was with her and she was too distraught to think about anything. She hadn't looked at anything, just found his phone and saw that he was gone. Now she was calmer and able to think about things.

She went straight to the cupboard in the

corner of the small living area and opened the door.

"His clothes are all still here," she said. "All except the ones he would have packed for the honeymoon. They were new, bought specially."

"Are you sure?"

"Yes. And here's his case."

She picked up the small suitcase which was wedged on the floor of the cupboard and lifted it up onto the bed. She opened it, flipping back the lid and showing the clothes inside, still with their tags on. She rummaged about in the sides of the case, took out the garments and searched in between each layer. She looked disappointed.

"What are you looking for?" Charlotte asked.

"The money," Samantha answered. "My father said he had left a parcel of cash here, the day before the wedding. A quarter of a million pounds." She flopped down onto the bed and caught back a sob. "He must have taken it with him. That means my father was right, doesn't it?"

Charlotte sat beside her and put her arm around her quivering shoulders. She was at a loss as to what to say to this heartbroken young girl, but she was sure her dilemma had a lot to do with the spirit of Miranda.

"Think about it, Samantha," she said. "If you were going out, even for a few minutes, you wouldn't leave that sort of cash lying around in this place, would you?"

"I suppose not. What are you saying?"

"I'm saying that just because the money is not here, doesn't mean your fiancé accepted it. He could have taken it with him with the intention of giving it back to your father."

"And he could have been mugged on the way, carrying that sort of cash around with him," Samantha said hopefully. "I bet that's what happened and he is lying injured somewhere. You see? I told you he hadn't left me."

CHAPTER FOUR

When they arrived back at Castle House, Charlotte let the dogs out of the people carrier and closed the door.

"I got some coffee, if you want some," she said.

"Yes please," Samantha replied, nodding eagerly. "Do you mind? I don't want to go home, not yet. I know what will happen; my father will be gloating, probably even organising a party so he can invite lots of suitable young men to take Simon's place."

Charlotte unlocked the front door and they went inside the house. The dogs went straight through and into the huge kitchen; it seemed the phantom had gone, at least for the time being.

She plugged in the kettle and spooned coffee into the mug for her guest.

"It's instant. I don't have any fancy machines; as I said, I don't drink the stuff. You know, that's what they used to do when this house was built, give huge gatherings to match up their daughters with suitable young men. They called them courts."

"That's where the term 'courting' came from?" Charlotte nodded. "If my father had his way, we would still be living in those times. He never liked Simon; he was always convinced he wasn't good enough."

"But you didn't believe it?"

Samantha shook her head.

"No. Simon didn't care about the money."

Charlotte made no reply. It was her experience that when someone said they didn't care about the money, it usually meant that they had so much of it they didn't have to care.

"You've been very kind," Samantha said. "I hope I'm not intruding too much. Will you be making another television programme?"

Charlotte smiled and shook her head.

"Not if I can help it. I only did that one to embarrass my husband."

"Oh. I didn't know you were married."

"I'm not, not any more at any rate. Aunt Florrie leaving me this place was a godsend as we were stuck with each other until the house sold. Even then he thought he was going to get a share."

"So you'll be staying?"

"I think so. I've always loved this place; it has so much history and it's been in the family for centuries. Besides, you and Mandy have got me intrigued. I too want to know what happened to Simon."

"So you believe me?" Charlotte nodded. "You're the only one who does."

"We'll have to see what we can do to change that. Being on television has its advantages; people tend to take more notice."

Samantha sipped at her coffee. It wasn't bad, considering it was instant and obviously the best she was going to get from her new friend.

Now she was really worried about Simon. He hadn't taken any of his clothes, so he had obviously intended to return to his flat. But what if he had taken the money? He wouldn't need his clothes then, would he? He'd have enough to buy new ones. She shook herself mentally, feeling like a traitor. He hadn't taken the money, he hadn't. She refused to believe it.

Samantha was certain something awful had happened to Simon. She loved him and she was sure he loved her. She had to cling to that thought.

"What shall I do now?" She asked.

"Well, Miranda didn't come here for no reason. She looked a bit battered about, but that doesn't really tell me anything. Do you know where she lived?"

"She has a little cottage in the High Street."

"Then drink up and we'll go there. But be prepared; we might just find her dead body."

***

It had been nearly a week since Charlotte packed all her things and left their London house and Peter was gradually coming to realise that he missed her. He hadn't really expected her to go, despite the divorce, and if that silly old woman hadn't left her Castle House she wouldn't have been able to.

That's what Peter had been depending on, that she would have nowhere to go and would have to stay. He had been secretly putting off prospective buyers; it wasn't difficult. All he'd had to do was make sure they came to view the house when he was there and Charlotte wasn't. She was always out in the morning walking the dogs, so he would arrange the viewings then, make sure he left the dog hairs about the place and point out how noisy the neighbours were.

He'd tell them they were lucky to have come at that time when the people next door were at work because in the evening their teenage son had his awful music going full blast. That was usually enough to send them scurrying back to the agent, with no intention of ever coming back.

They had bought this house when they married and Peter didn't want to sell it. That crafty old cow had waited for the divorce to be finalised before changing her Will and leaving Castle House and all her money to Charlotte and she'd done it deliberately so that Peter would have no say in the disposal of it.

It was worth millions. They could start again with that sort of money, they could pay off the mortgage on this place, take a long holiday, even buy a small yacht to keep on the Thames. He smiled to himself. Now that was a thought; they could rent this place out, move down to Surrey and get one of those big houses that backed onto the Thames. They could keep a boat there, right on the back doorstep and they would be very comfortable. He could give up work and she could forget all this spiritualist nonsense.

On the other hand, Castle House would thrive as a hotel. He'd mentioned it to her, but only briefly, yet it was a solution if she really didn't want to part with it. His own job was getting a bit too pressurised just lately, with all the graduates coming in with all the qualifications but no experience. And Peter wasn't getting any younger. Why, in his profession, mid thirties was practically a senior citizen.

He imagined him and Charlotte together, entertaining the guests, showing them around the house and pointing out the history. They'd make a fortune. Charlotte was a wonderful cook, even though she pretended she didn't enjoy it. All women enjoyed cooking, didn't they? They wouldn't even need to employ a chef, at least not straight away.

Without the pressure of his job and in a new place where nobody knew about her, they could make a go of it.

Of course, she'd already been on television, but it was unlikely people in that part of the country would have seen her.

He suddenly felt a flutter of excitement. He needed to see Charlotte, needed to put his scheme to her seriously and make her see how they could make it work.

He went upstairs, threw a few shirts and pants into a small suitcase and grabbed his car keys. It was Saturday and it was time he treated himself to a long weekend.

***

Miranda's little cottage was one of those old labourer's dwellings that had once been part of a large estate. The door opened straight onto the pavement and the windows were low, so that anyone walking passed could see inside. If a person was inside, they would see lots of legs walking past; Charlotte felt depressed just looking at it. It looked deserted, but appearances could be deceptive.

Charlotte opened the vehicle's windows for the dogs and told them to stay, then she climbed out of the driver's seat and turned to her passenger.

"Are you ready for this?" She asked.

Samantha drew in a deep breath to give her courage, still not really sure whether to believe that Mandy was dead. She didn't really want to go inside the cottage, didn't want to knock on the door and be faced with the girl who had caused so much trouble ever since she met Simon. She had done everything she could think of to try to separate them and she was bound to have heard about the farce that was their wedding day. Now she would more than likely be thrilled to gloat about it and laugh at Samantha's gullibility.

Charlotte knocked on the door, using the heavy, metal knocker that looked as old as the cottage itself. There was a presence inside this cottage, Charlotte could feel it even through the closed door, but she was sure it wasn't Miranda.

She heard a voice, a voice speaking in old Cornish, a language now dead and mostly forgotten. She couldn't understand what the voice was saying, but it was a man's voice. It was probably the spirit of whoever was once the tenant of this cottage, perhaps some two or three hundred years ago.

She glanced at Samantha. No, she had heard nothing; Charlotte hadn't really expected her to. Those who had been in spirit as long as this fella were never apparent to the ordinary folk, only to people like Charlotte who had been seeing and hearing them all her life.

She moved to the window and peered inside, shielding her eyes with her hands against the glass. There wasn't much to see, just some sparse furniture and a television set. It was a very tiny room and wouldn't have held much more.

This cottage was the last in the row so she made her way around the side, Samantha following, to see if there was a back entrance. There was and it was unlocked.

Inside was tidy, the washing up draining on

the wooden board beside the old bucket sink and through a low doorway was the little living room into which Charlotte had peered. Samantha made her way up the narrow, rickety staircase and into the one bedroom.

She opened the wardrobe and her heart sank.

"Find anything?" Charlotte called out from the bottom of the stairs.

"Yes. All the cupboards and drawers are empty; all her clothes have gone. She had no intention of coming back."

"Not much to see here then," Charlotte said. At least not much that was still of this world. "It's getting late and the baby bears need their dinner. We'll give up for tonight; it's possible my visitor might have found her voice and can tell us more tomorrow."

***

When Samantha got home, the first thing she noticed was the absence of all the wedding gifts. The table that had held them had been folded down to its smaller size, the middle panel dropped down and out of sight. All that remained on its surface was a huge vase of roses which had come for her that morning from an ex-boyfriend, a wealthy one whom her father favoured.

No doubt he had got in touch with him and others to inform them that his lovely daughter was back on the market, like some object of value for which they could bid.

"What have you done?" She demanded. "I said I didn't want them to go back."

Her mother got up from the armchair where she had been reading and hurried to comfort her.

"I know you did, darling, but it had to be done. It was beginning to look bad."

"Oh, well, we have to get our priorities right, don't we?"

On the marble mantelpiece was an opened envelope, addressed to Samantha. Her mother picked it up and handed it to her.

"We found this among all the cards that came on the day of the wedding."

"You opened it? It is addressed to me, and you opened it?"

"That's right," her father's voice came from behind her. "We opened all of them. We didn't want you to be upset."

That was too much! They were her cards, her gifts. They had no right to interfere. But she knew they were trying to spare her more heartache so, despite being angry, she accepted it.

The name on the envelope was written in a hand she recognised but she didn't want to admit it. It wasn't a card; it wasn't thick enough to be a card but she could easily guess what it was.

She took the envelope and pulled out the letter from inside. Her heart twisted as she read the contents, but there was something about the writing in the letter that was different from that which had written her name on the envelope. Or was that just wishful thinking? It was similar enough to be the same and it was possible it had just been written with more care than usual. She could see no other reason for her doubts.

Sorry, Samantha, it read. *It's obvious we come from two different worlds and I realised that Miranda was right; I belong with her. Have a nice life and thank your dad for the money. Simon.*

She shook her head. This was not happening; this could definitely not be happening. She crunched the letter up in her hand, tears began to gather in her eyes as she raised them to look at her parents, at the smugness her father couldn't hide.

Her mother sat in her usual armchair beside the huge, marble fireplace and looked down at her hands, so Samantha couldn't see her expression. She had supported Samantha throughout, ever since the engagement her mother had appeared to be on her side, even while trying to gently convince her that Simon was not the right man for her.

Even since the day of the wedding, she had been able to go to her for comfort, but she'd never actually come out and said she was sorry for her. Samantha thought it likely she didn't want to go against her husband; she was old fashioned that way.

But something was wrong and she knew it, even if they didn't. She crunched the letter up into a ball as she grabbed her bag and her car keys from the side cupboard and headed towards the door.

"Where are you going?" Her mother called after her.

"I'm going to stay with a friend," she called back. "I cannot stand to see *his* smug face everywhere I look."

She didn't have to elaborate on whose face; that was obvious. He had won; he had finally found Simon's price and now he could look forward to knowing it.

"You shouldn't be driving that car," her mother shouted. "Not in that state! Please."

"Tell him," Samantha called back just before she slammed the door. "He bought the damned thing."

Sarah Montfield was probably right, Samantha had to admit. She hated this car even in the best of moods, and the way she felt right now, she would be safer in a space capsule. But she wasn't about to let her father know that.

She started the ignition and rammed the gear lever into first, took off along the coast road without a clue as to where she was going.

Staying with a friend, she had told Sarah, but that wasn't her intention at all. She didn't want to tell her friends what had happened; she didn't think they would be smug about it, but you never knew. Secretly, she was sure, they had been just as suspicious of Simon as Jason had, although they never said so. It was human nature for a person to be pleased when they were proved right, wasn't it?

She could go to a hotel for a few nights. Then she wouldn't have to talk to anyone, wouldn't have to admit to anyone that she'd been made a complete fool of.

She remembered all the expensive gifts she'd bought for Simon since she'd known him, remembered that she had put a huge chunk of her own allowance into his business.

He'd said he didn't want anything, but she had insisted. She wanted him to succeed and the loan he would have needed from the bank would have crippled him before he started. That was a secret between her and Simon; she never intended her parents to find out about it.

She pulled up in a layby on the cliff's edge and pulled her handbag onto her lap, opened it and looked into her purse. A few pounds in cash and a whole load of credit and debit cards. And if she used any one of those, Jason would be able to track where she was. He had enough clout to persuade anyone to do anything.

She got out and slammed the door, walked

around to the front of the car and looked down at the beach far below. Far out to sea was one wave which was higher than the rest of the ocean, a wave which would be enormous when it reached the shore. It would be great for surfers, but there weren't any about at this time of year.

There was a woman down there, a dark haired woman with two enormous, fluffy dogs, one black and one brown, playing in the waves like children.

"Charlotte," she murmured to herself.

Suddenly she felt better; not much but definitely better. Charlotte had been kind to her, had believed her when no one else would. Perhaps she would let her stay for a few days, let her pour out her heart and advise her of the best way to move forward.

She was waiting when Charlotte returned to the house with her dogs, who came hurtling towards her to say hello. Samantha knew by now that they would not knock her over, that they didn't jump up and would stop when they got close and she reached out her hands to stroke them both. They were wet and smelly from their paddle in the sea.

Strangely enough, until she met Charlotte, she had no idea she liked dogs. She'd never had one, never wanted one, but if it wasn't for the hair and the drool, she could have lived with one of these giants.

"Come in," Charlotte said as she opened the front door. "Did you bring a change of knickers or do you need to go shopping?"

"How did you know?"

Charlotte shrugged.

"I just do. Something drastic has happened and I'm the only one you've come across in this miserable business who believes you." She paused and gestured to Samantha's swollen face. "Besides, you've been crying again."

She found Charlotte something of an enigma. She wasn't sure whether half of what she said was psychic ability or just observation, but it hardly mattered. She'd proved right so far, all except Mandy's ghost anyway. That couldn't be right, could it? Not considering the contents of Simon's letter.

Samantha pulled the crushed up note from her handbag where she'd put it when she arrived, along with its envelope, and tossed it onto the kitchen table, while Charlotte switched on the kettle to make them hot drinks. It was getting chilly now and was really cold down on the beach, but the dogs loved the cold.

She'd had time to look around the house properly, to see what Aunt Florrie had left and how much there was to explore, and she knew she would be happy here.

She gave Samantha her coffee and sat down with her tea. She pulled the paper straight, pressed it out with her fingers and read it. She felt sorry for Samantha, but there was something wrong with this letter and she was reluctant to say so. She needed time to study it, to feel the energy left behind by the writer. She didn't want to build her hopes up, but there was only one way to learn the truth and Samantha would have to face it.

"Tell me," she said. "When I asked you who Miranda was, you said she was always called Mandy. Did Simon call her Mandy, or did her use her full name?"

"Mandy," she answered. "I don't think he even knew her full name."

"Then why would he write it as Miranda in this note?"

Samantha shook her head.

"I don't know. Perhaps it was what she wanted. What difference does it make? It means my father was right all along and it means that you were wrong. Mandy is not dead; she is enjoying herself with my fiancé, spending the quarter of a million pounds my father paid him to go away. I was a fool, a stupid, lovesick, helpless idiot and I shall never trust a man again as long as I live."

The tears began to gather again as Charlotte studied the letter more closely. Mandy, Miranda, whatever her name was, she was no longer in this world and Charlotte was certain of that.

The dogs finished their water and came to their mistress to have their mouths wiped, then they headed for the hallway and took up their position at the bottom of the stairs.

"They're doing it again," Samantha said.

"Yes. She's back."

"But she can't be. She's alive and well and somewhere with Simon."

Charlotte shook her head.

"I don't think so. I'm sorry, Samantha; I don't want to build your hopes but I know for certain she is now in spirit and she is trying desperately to tell me something."

CHAPTER FIVE

It was Freya who abandoned her surveillance of the staircase to race toward the front door and bark. Fritz followed, but kept silent. It was always the way; she was the guard dog of the two, if one could ever call a Newfie such a thing.

Charlotte looked out of the front window and sighed wearily.

"Who's that?" Samantha asked. "Is it my father?"

"No. It is my ex-husband."

She opened the door and the dogs ran out, their tails wagging happily as they pressed their furry bodies close to Peter. He put up his hands in a gesture of surrender. They were still damp and he obviously didn't want them too close. When they moved away from him, he began to walk toward the house, toward Charlotte.

"What are you doing here?" She asked.

He gave her that smile, the smile that used to be able to melt her heart and persuade her to anything. She was relieved to find it had little effect. He leaned forward to kiss her cheek, but thankfully took the hint when she pulled her face away.

"We need to talk."

"Why? Have you sold the house? You need me to sign something? You could have posted it."

"Not yet, no. I've had a few thoughts about that and I'd like to talk to you about them. Aren't you going to ask me in?"

"It wasn't my intention, no."

"Come on, Charlotte. I've come a long way; I could do with a drink."

He eyed Samantha's Porsche appreciatively. It didn't seem like the sort of car Charlotte would buy, especially as it wasn't big enough for her precious dogs, but you never knew. He freely admitted he knew little about her really. She had accused him of trying to mould her to his ideas and she was right. That would all change now.

"Nice car," he said. "Florrie must have left you more than you expected."

What the hell was he talking about? Charlotte allowed her gaze to follow his and she grinned, but did not correct him. Let him think the Porsche was hers; it wouldn't do her any harm.

Inside she poured him tea from the pot already made and handed it to him.

"Don't you have anything stronger?" He asked.

"The only alcohol in our house was the stuff you bought," she answered curtly. "Or was that something else about me that went over your head?"

"Let's not get off on the wrong foot, Charlotte. That television producer phoned, wanting to know if you'd be prepared to sign up for another

TV show. I told him you wouldn't be interested."

"You did? Why? Did you think perhaps I wouldn't be, or is that what you wanted?"

He looked about the kitchen with the same appreciation in his eyes that he'd had for the Porsche. Take out this enormous table and this kitchen was easily big enough to cook for more than just a family. They could fit a big, catering sized cooker in there, get a bigger fridge. It was ideal.

His glance fell on the enormous garden at the back that dropped down to the beach at the end. And there were the castle ruins. He'd forgotten about that. Those ruins would draw in more visitors.

He could see it all taking shape in his mind. It would be a five star hotel and it would get into the top hotel guides and they could charge a fortune for a room. They wouldn't have any riff raff, would they? Not at those prices. Oh, this was going to be so good.

"Well, we don't need it, do we?" He said at last, dragging his attention back to the call from the television producer. "This place is worth a fortune. I told you that before but you weren't in the mood to listen. Have you had it valued yet? You should, if only for the insurance."

We don't need it?

She hated to admit that he was right about the insurance, and not something she had thought of. If, God forbid, there was a fire, it would be a major disaster and some of the fittings and furniture went back to the fourteenth century, from the original castle.

As soon as she managed to get rid of him, she'd find an insurance company on the internet and get it sorted.

"Anyway, Charlotte, I've been giving the matter serious thought. If you don't want to sell the place, and I can understand that, think what a great hotel it would make. All that history, even the castle ruins in the back garden and right on the beach." He drained his mug and put it back on the table. "What do you think?"

Charlotte opened a drawer behind her and pulled out a heavy piece of paper, tossed it across the table to Peter.

"You see that?" She said. "That is headed Decree Absolute. That means there is no 'we', there is just you and me, you in London me three hundred miles away in Cornwall. You can be content in the knowledge that your wife will no longer embarrass you, talking to dead folks and making a fool of herself."

"Charlotte, please. I came all this way hoping we could start again. With the money we could make, running our own hotel here, you'll have plenty of time for those two." He nodded toward the hall, to where Fritz and Freya had once more taken up their position at the bottom of the stairs. "We could even start a family."

Charlotte laughed out loud at that. Peter had never wanted children, something else he didn't bother to tell her before they married, but now he was thinking of getting his feet back under the table he was prepared to offer even that. He wouldn't go through with it, of course. Once he got his way, he would find reasons to put it off. Not that she intended to give him the chance.

She was rather surprised to find that she cared nothing for him anymore, that the love she had once had for him had dissolved over the years of his continual efforts to make her suppress what she really was.

"Peter, I don't want to argue with you. There's a good hotel about a mile away where you can probably get a room for the night, being as it's out of season, then you can drive back to London in the morning."

"But we need to talk."

"What about? The only reason you're suddenly interested is because of Aunt Florrie's inheritance. I'm not going into the hotel trade and I'm not coming back to you. It's time for you to move on."

"Not without you."

"Where does whatsername fit into this plan of yours?"

"If you mean Rachel, she doesn't. When the divorce came through she wanted us to get married and I suddenly realised I didn't want to be married to anyone but you. Doesn't that tell you something?"

"Yes. It tells me you've missed your chance. Now go, please, before I lose my temper."

A whoof from Freya sent Charlotte to the window once more. *What now?* All she wanted was time alone with Miranda's ghost, to try to get more information out of her, but it seemed that was not to be.

Samantha had politely taken herself off when Peter arrived and Charlotte had no idea where she was, hopefully exploring the house or the grounds, somewhere safe.

Standing on her doorstep this time was Jason Montfield, wearing a face like thunder.

"I want my daughter," he demanded.

"Really? I don't think she wants you, but I will ask."

"I've already phoned the police, so you can forget trying to hide her."

Charlotte rolled her eyes at the sky.

"Don't the police have anything better to do than run around after you?" She turned toward the staircase, saw that Miranda was still there, still looking worried, and called up the stairs. "Samantha! Your father has decided to join the party."

She hadn't bothered to shut the door. She knew that Fritz and Freya would never let anyone through the door unless she had invited them and now they stood on the threshold, barring the way. She noticed Jason Montfield didn't try to force his way passed them and that made her smile. It always surprised her how many people were afraid to cross these two purely because of their size.

She didn't want to invite this man in, but it seemed the easiest way.

"You may as well come in," she said.

Immediately the two huge dogs turned to Charlotte and sat themselves in front of her. It was their way of protecting her, so she concluded they sensed a threat of some kind. But her attention was immediately drawn to the phantom on the half landing, who was growing more and more agitated as Jason Montfield passed the dogs as he made his way across the hallway.

She was pointing at him, her eyes wide and frightened, her mouth opening and closing but no sound coming out.

Whatever had happened to Miranda, Charlotte was sure this man had something to do with it.

"Father, what do you want?" Samantha passed through Miranda's image to reach the bottom of the stairs then brushed passed the dogs to stand in front of her father.

"You lied to me," he said. "You said you were staying with friends. I phoned every one of them before I found out you'd been hanging around with this charlatan."

Charlotte raised an eyebrow. She'd been

called worse and his opinion was of no interest to her.

"Charlotte is my friend," Samantha said. "She is the only one who would listen to me."

"Why? How much is she charging?" He turned an angry face to Charlotte, his fists clenched. "I can see how it was. She arrived here, heard the local gossip about the wedding and thought she could make a few bob out of it. How much have you paid her so far?"

"Nothing," Samantha said. "She has charged me nothing. In fact, I probably owe her for all the free meals she has provided."

"Well, you wait and see," Jason insisted. "It won't be long before she cons you into making a donation."

He took a threatening step toward Charlotte as he spoke but he got no closer. Fritz and Freya positioned themselves closer together, their huge heads resting just above her waist, and stared at him. He moved back, looking fearfully at the dogs, then he turned back to Samantha.

"Come on," he said. "You're coming home with me."

The sound of a car on the driveway caught Charlotte's attention. It seemed she was not to be allowed any peace, but this visitor was no threat to her.

"Did you say something about phoning the police, Mr Montfield?" Charlotte asked. "I think they have arrived."

That is when Peter decided it was safe to show his face. He emerged from the kitchen and went to open the front door, to let the police inside. Did he think Charlotte wouldn't notice that he only got involved when there was police back up.

The dogs didn't leave Charlotte to go to the door, not this time. They obviously thought their services were needed here.

***

Detective Sergeant Paul Middleton was not in the best of moods when he pulled up in the driveway of Castle House.

Anyone else would have got a uniformed constable, if anyone at all, but Jason Montfield snapped his fingers and the whole damned police force were supposed to respond.

His daughter was here, he said, in the home of the television spiritualist, Charlotte Chase. She must be being held against her will. Yeah, right. He had far more important cases to work on than a summons from the local multi-millionaire and his spoilt daughter.

Paul had heard all about her recent upset, he could hardly have missed it, and it was not unheard of for someone to consult a medium in such traumatic circumstances. She probably wanted to be reassured that her fiancé was still alive. Or perhaps she wanted to be assured that he was not, since being dead was probably the only excuse she would accept for his jilting her at the altar.

Either way, she was a consenting adult, Charlotte Chase was well known and had no criminal record, so valuable police resources being employed to investigate made him mad. When it came to the law, Paul was very much in favour of the same laws for everyone, no matter who they were or how much they were worth.

Still, he couldn't deny he was glad of the opportunity to get inside Castle House. He had lived in this town all his life and had often passed this place and gazed longingly at it.

He'd always wanted to have a look round, but everyone knew Miss Mason was something of a recluse and he'd never quite got up the nerve to ask her.

He got out of his car and looked into the distance at the ruins of the castle rising up on the edge of the garden, just before it dropped down to the beach. What an amazing place this was. He'd heard that it was built in the time of Queen Elizabeth I and his love of history made him volunteer for this assignment. He hoped he got a chance to explore.

He certainly hadn't come to interfere with the civil rights of a consenting adult, which Samantha Montfield was.

The scene which met his eyes when a man opened the door was definitely not what he was expecting. He recognised Charlotte Chase, standing in the large hallway with two of the most enormous dogs he had ever seen sitting in front of her as though guarding her against any threat to her safety.

In front of them was Jason Montfield, the multi-millionaire who could say the word and have the whole police force do his bidding. And he looked threatening all right; he stood with one foot slightly in front of the other as though about to lunge forward and his fists were clenched.

In front of him stood a young woman, whom Paul assumed was Montfield's 'kidnapped' daughter, although she certainly didn't look as though she were in any danger. In fact, were it not for those dogs, Paul felt sure Charlotte Chase would have been the one in danger.

"Thank God you've arrived," Jason said at once, turning to face the detective. "Now you can arrest this lunatic and take my daughter home."

"Dad," Samantha said. "I am here of my own free will and Charlotte has been helping me."

"Helping you? How much for?"

"You think everything is about you and your money, don't you? Well, it isn't."

Paul sighed heavily. It was as he thought, another rich man trying to control everything with his wealth.

"Miss Montfield," he said. "May I ask your

age?"

"I am nineteen, why? Why is that important?"

"Because you are an adult and if you say you are here willingly, as far as I can see the only one breaking the law is your father."

"What? I'll have your job for that."

Paul chose to ignore the remark.

"Miss Chase," he said. "Do you want Mr Montfield here in your house?"

"No. I don't want him either," she gestured toward Peter.

"Then, Mr Montfield, I must ask you to leave before I arrest you for threatening behaviour. As to this other gentleman, I don't know what he's supposed to have done. Is he with you?"

"No, he's not."

He looked at Charlotte who shrugged.

"He's my ex-husband, Sergeant. He's broken no law, unless being stupid is illegal."

"All right," Jason said. "I'll leave, but not without my daughter."

"She doesn't have to go with you, Sir," Paul said. "Now, are you going to leave Miss Chase's property, or am I going to arrest you?"

"You'll be sorry for this, young man. Be certain of it."

Paul made no reply. It was pointless trying to argue with a man like this; he would always have the last word, even if that last word was irrelevant. He watched him leave, went to the door and saw him climb into the driver's seat of his Aston Martin and drove away.

"Thank you, Sergeant," Charlotte said.

The dogs left their position and went to the living room where they climbed on separate sofas and settled down to sleep. Their mistress was no longer in danger; now they could relax.

"If you are okay, Miss Chase, I'll get back to the police station. I have a body to identify, which is unusual in this part of the world."

"Whose body?" Samantha asked quickly.

Paul could see by the fear in her wide eyes that she thought it might be her missing bridegroom. He almost wished he could tell it was; at least then she could move on with her life.

"I shouldn't discuss the case, Miss," he said. "But I can tell you it is that of a woman."

CHAPTER SIX

When the police officer had gone Charlotte opened the internet and looked up the address of the hotel along the coast, wrote it down for Peter and sent him on his away, protesting all the way out of the door.

"I'll pop back tomorrow," he said. "When you've had time to think about things. We could make a wonderful hotel out of this place."

"I don't think so, Peter," Charlotte answered. "The ghosts might scare away the guests."

Peter sighed, bit his lip to hold back a retort.

"We could make a fortune."

"Peter, let's get this straight, shall we? I have no desire to go into any business with you and I have no intention of reconciling with you. Aunt Florrie had everything marked down in her Will to leave to various animal sanctuaries, just so you wouldn't get your hands on it. As soon as the divorce was final, she changed that Will. If I were to let you into any part of it, I know she would come back to haunt us."

Again he bit his lip in frustration, but he drove away. Charlotte could only hope he realised she was a lost cause and she would never see him again.

Her next task was to phone the local Chinese takeaway and order a delivery. One of the few concessions to the twenty first century this remote part of the world made was a Chinese takeaway. She went back on the internet to arrange that house insurance. She hadn't thought of it, but now she had, she wouldn't sleep until it was done.

She fed the dogs then settled down to wait and study Samantha's letter in more detail. When she'd first touched it, she knew at once there was something not right, but the interference of first Peter then Jason Montfield had left her with no opportunity to study further.

She heard the kettle switch and turned to smile at Samantha. She was trying to make herself useful, poor girl, and Charlotte could see she'd been crying again. Even if Simon did turn out to be a conman, Samantha didn't love him any less.

"What are you thinking?" Samantha asked, sitting down at the table.

"The envelope is fancy, looks as though it was designed to match whatever was inside, possibly a card or something. But the paper on the letter is a different colour and not even of the same quality."

"So you think the envelope is genuine, but Simon wrote the letter afterwards?"

Charlotte shook her head.

"I don't think Simon wrote this letter at all," she said. She took Samantha's hand and squeezed it. "I don't want to build your hopes up and I'm no expert, but it seems to me the writing in the letter is not natural and I can see the hand that wrote it."

"You can?"

"It was a woman's hand. Do you have anything that Simon wrote, besides this envelope?"

"No," Samantha replied. "Simon wasn't one for writing. He only did what he had to for the business but even that was a struggle."

"He's dyslexic?"

"Yes. Something else my father had against him. But you didn't refer to him in the past tense."

Charlotte looked at her thoughtfully, wondering how much she should reveal. This girl didn't need any more disappointments.

"Simon is not dead," she said. "I would know, but whether that means he is genuine or not, I couldn't say. But if he is dyslexic, he definitely didn't write this letter."

"Perhaps it was Mandy who wrote it. She's the only one who would have given herself her full name."

"Tell me, you say she stalked you and Simon. Did she ever approach your parents?"

"Once. She came to the house when I was out with Simon; my mother told me." She paused thoughtfully for a moment. "Come to think of it, she referred to her as Miranda, so that's what she said her name was. Mum never knew her as Mandy."

"That makes sense," Charlotte said with a note of hesitation. "The hand I see writing this is not a young one. It is older, much older and it wears a diamond ring, surrounded by little rubies."

Samantha sat up sharply, her whole body going rigid.

"Are you sure?" She asked, her lips quivering and an ache in her throat that threatened to choke her.

"I rather wish I wasn't. You recognise the description?"

"That ring," she said. "It never leaves my mother's finger. It belonged to my grandmother." Those tears started up again and Charlotte squeezed her hand. "She said she understood, that she knew what it was to be in love. I thought she was on my side at least, but apparently not. They've done something to Simon."

The heavy medieval door knocker rattled, taking Freya to the front door barking, Fritz following but keeping silent.

"That'll be our dinner," Charlotte said.

"I'm not sure I feel like eating now."

Charlotte opened the door to the delivery driver and was surprised to see Detective Sergeant Middleton standing beside him.

She paid for the takeaway, then stepped back

to allow Paul to enter. Charlotte wondered what he was doing back here, but she was hungry and was not about to delay her meal to answer his questions.

In the kitchen, Samantha was laying out plates.

"Will you join us, Sergeant?" Charlotte asked.

"I'm tempted. I haven't eaten all day, thanks to..." He glanced at Samantha and his voice trailed off.

"Thanks to my father wasting police time," she said. "I hope you're going to charge him with that."

"I would love to, Miss, believe me, but my superiors have other ideas."

Samantha got another plate out of the cupboard and set it on the table.

"Are you sure about this?" Paul asked.

"There's always too much for me," Charlotte replied. "And I don't let the baby bears have this sort of stuff; it's bad for their digestion."

It didn't do a lot for Paul's digestion either, but this woman seemed far more concerned with her dogs than any humans. He was a dog lover and he had to admit, they were magnificent.

They approached the table to see what might be on offer, laid their chins on the surface with no effort at all but when Charlotte looked at them and pointed to the kitchen door, they took themselves off. Paul wondered how much training that had taken; or was it that she had some psychic link with them?

"What can I do for you, Sergeant?" Charlotte asked as she ate.

"It's Miss Montfield I came to see. You remember I mentioned a body? Well, it was discovered in a ditch the other side of Porthgowan. We think you might know the victim."

"You said it was a woman," Samantha said, suddenly afraid they had found Simon.

"That's right, Miss. It was."

"Was it an accident of some sort?"

"No. We are fairly sure the woman was murdered and dumped there. She had no identification, no driving licence, bank cards, nothing, so whoever dumped her there didn't intend that she should be identified."

"And how did you identify her, Sergeant?" Charlotte asked.

She already knew who the victim was; there was no other reason for the spirit to be visiting.

"She had breast implants," Paul answered, shovelling rice into his mouth. "They have serial numbers."

He was eating as though food was going to be hard to come by and really wanted nothing more than to finish his meal.

A short laugh came from Samantha.

"You find that amusing, Miss Montfield?"

"She had those implants at the same time as she dyed her hair dark brown to match mine.

She also had dark brown contact lenses, although she didn't need them. She did everything she could to try to look like me and I have a generous bust."

"You know who the victim is then?"

"It sounds like Mandy." She tossed the letter across the table to Paul. "I got this; Charlotte thinks it's not Simon's writing and I agree."

He swallowed the last bite of his meal and picked up the letter. Was he now going to act upon the word of a psychic? He needed something more than that.

"What makes you think so?" He asked.

Samantha opened her mouth to tell him about the hand that wrote the letter, but Charlotte gripped her wrist to get her attention. She wanted to keep the information in this world, not the next. Otherwise it would be dismissed and they would be no closer to finding Simon.

"The paper is all wrong. It doesn't match the envelope. I think the seal has been steamed open and resealed using glue of some sort. Samantha tells me that no one ever called her 'Miranda' except herself and that Simon was dyslexic, so it seems unlikely that he wrote this letter."

"Is it possible he faked being dyslexic? It could all have been part of the plan to marry you and gain access to your father's fortune. The Chief Inspector has interviewed him already and he says he gave your fiancé a quarter of a million pounds in cash. We are thinking that once he had the money, he decided he didn't need Miranda any more."

"No!"

Samantha jumped to her feet, her fists were clenched in anger and her complexion was crimson.

"Simon didn't kill her! Why the hell should he? He could have gone abroad with that money, changed his name even and she'd never have been able to find him. If he wanted to kill her he would have done it months ago, when she was following us about and causing trouble everywhere we went. Simon wouldn't hurt a soul."

"All right, Miss Montfield," Paul said. "It's just a theory we're pursuing."

"Then you're wasting your time. Simon didn't write that letter and neither did Mandy."

"Sergeant," Charlotte interrupted before her guest could tell him about her vision. "Have you tried Simon's workshop, to see if there is anything there to confirm your theory?"

Samantha rummaged in her handbag and tossed the keys to the workshop across the table.

"Help yourself. He has nothing to hide."

"What about his family?" Paul asked. "We need to interview them."

"He has no family," Samantha answered miserably. "He was in care until he was eighteen, then he got a job as a trainee mechanic and worked his way up. He has no one but me.

And he is not a killer!"

"Thank you, Miss Montfield. I'll get these back to you." Paul stood up to leave. "Thanks for the meal, Miss Chase. I really needed that."

Charlotte studied him carefully. He was about her age, tall, well built. Had Peter not put her off men, she could go for this one.

"That's perfectly all right, Sergeant. You can return the favour some time." She followed him to the door. "Where did you say Miranda's body was found?"

"The other side of Porthgowan in a ditch on the main A389. Why?"

"Just wondering."

"Look, Miss Chase…"

"Charlotte, please."

"All right, Charlotte. I hope you're not planning on doing your own investigating in this matter. We have to be extra careful, with the connection to Jason Montfield."

"Sergeant, if Simon is alive, and I am certain that he is, he could be in trouble and he is likely to be near to where you found Miranda's body. That note wasn't written by him and it wasn't written by her, but I believe it might have been dictated by her. No one else called her Miranda."

"What do you know?"

"Nothing you'd want to know about, I'm sure."

"Charlotte, others might scoff at your abilities but not me. I know there are people who can sense things, even see things and if you know something, you need to tell me."

Charlotte hesitated for a moment. Should she trust him? At last she shrugged; what had she got to lose after all?

"Very well. That letter was written by a woman but not Miranda, an older woman. She was wearing a ring that Samantha is sure belongs to her mother. If Miranda told her what to write, and I believe she did, it was on a promise."

"A promise of what? Money?"

"No. I don't feel that. She was crazy about Simon, stalked him, tried her best to split him and Samantha up. I think perhaps she was persuaded that if she helped forge the letter, Simon would be hers, along with a quarter of a million pounds."

"Why are you so sure he didn't write it?"

"I told you; he's dyslexic and look at the writing. It's forced, contrived, as though copied from something. But they only had the one word to copy from. I think the idea was to use Miranda to make it look as though he had taken off with her. Now she is dead and I believe he is in danger of being the same."

CHAPTER SEVEN

The drive to Porthgowan was not a long one and all the time Charlotte was thinking of how many places there were around that area to hide a kidnap victim. She also wondered why Miranda's killers hadn't dumped her body on the Moor; it might never have been found had they done so, but for some reason they'd just turfed it out of their car and into a ditch.

Charlotte assumed that was what had happened anyway and she thought it likely that it was because they didn't want to be seen going up to the Moor.

Then there was Porthgowan Gaol, that gruesome place that Charlotte had long ago boycotted. It was open to the public but there were parts that were still closed off and it had more ghosts than anywhere else she'd ever been. They were not happy ghosts either, not spirits who just didn't want to leave what they were used to; these were angry spirits, malevolent ones.

Some were criminals rightfully convicted and hanged, and were still angry about being caught, but others were innocent, condemned to death on the flimsiest of evidence and they cried out for justice.

They left Charlotte feeling distraught and

trying her hardest to convince them to move on, but they never seemed to hear her and there was nothing she could do about it.

There was one young man who had been hanged for the murder of his girlfriend; the locals had been so sure he was guilty, they'd even put up a memorial stone on the spot where her body was found, naming him as her killer and they had done it before the trial. He'd had no chance and Charlotte knew for certain he was innocent.

It seemed likely she had committed suicide but the family would rather see an innocent man hanged than admit to the shame of such a thing. That case had really distressed her and she hoped she wouldn't be led to that awful place.

But she had a strong feeling that was precisely where she would be led. Miranda's spirit had calmed down since her remains were discovered, but she was still hanging about which meant her needs had not yet been met.

Was she waiting for them to find Simon? Probably.

They passed the Porthgowan sign and Charlotte headed towards the Moor and that was when both dogs began to bark in the back of the people carrier. It was very rare for either of them to bark while travelling and even rarer for Fritz to bark at all.

Samantha twisted around in her seat and put out a hand to sooth the two huge dogs.

"What's wrong, darlings?" She asked.

But Charlotte knew the answer. She glanced in the rear view mirror and saw the cause of their agitation. Miranda had decided to make this journey with them.

"Ok, Babies," she said soothingly. "I see her."

"Who? Mandy?"

Charlotte nodded.

"She is in the back and she is telling us we are going the wrong way. That's just what I was afraid of."

The transparent image in the back of Charlotte's vehicle was pointing toward the road which led away from the Moor and to the Gaol. Damn!

Miranda faded away as Charlotte pulled up into the car park and found a parking space outside the main doors. There was no sun, thank goodness. The doors were solid wood, very thick and encased in iron bars and sharp studs.

She got out and let the dogs out to relieve themselves, then she put them back inside, opened the windows and shut the doors.

"Where are we?" Samantha asked.

"Porthgowan Gaol," Charlotte replied. "I haven't been here in years and I hoped never to come here again, but this is where he is."

Samantha gripped Charlotte's sleeve as her hopes soared.

"Simon?" She said. "Are you sure?"

"Miranda is sure; that's good enough for me."

***

"She's gone from one parasite straight into the arms of another," Jason Montfield said angrily. "How much will it cost to buy this one off, I wonder?"

"Calm down, darling," his wife, Sarah said soothingly. She put her hand gently on his arm and kissed his cheek. "This isn't the same thing at all. She's turned to this woman for comfort and perhaps she's able to give it. Who knows? At least you managed to get rid of Simple Simon; he has, as you thought, taken the money and run. Give her time."

"I thought she had more sense."

"She does. But her heart is broken; she has not only lost the man she thought she loved, she has discovered he was a con artist, only after enough money to run away with this other girl. And he was good at it, too. He had this Mandy turn up all over the place, never leaving him alone, drawing our girl even closer in."

Jason looked down at his wife, where her head rested on his upper arm and he forced a smile. She was right; Simple Simon wasn't so simple after all was he? He could have done with someone like that working for him.

The doorbell rang, making Jason sigh impatiently.

"What the hell now?" He demanded of the air

around him. "If that is reporters, they'll wish they hadn't bothered."

They'd been pestered by reporters after the wedding farce, but since Samantha had got herself involved with a television medium for God's sake, they'd be buzzing round liked flies on a dead carcass. It was bound to get out; there could be no stopping it, not in a town this size.

But there were no reporters standing on his doorstep when he opened the door. Instead it was the police sergeant who'd had the effrontery to tell him he had no right to take his daughter home.

"What do you want?" He demanded of the young man.

"I would like you to answer some questions, Sir," Detective Sergeant Middleton replied. "May I come in? Or do you want to come to the station?"

"How dare you? And how dare they send a sergeant to me. If the police have questions, they can send a senior officer."

Paul sighed. Bloody rich people thought they could dictate everything. He didn't begrudge them the money, only the ideas it gave them.

"The station then," Paul said, stepping back. "Do you want to get a jacket? It's cold out."

Jason realised this could be done much quicker if he just invited the copper inside, although he couldn't imagine what he wanted.

"All right," he said, moving back to make

room. "Come in. But be quick. My wife and I have a lot to take care of."

In the sitting room Paul looked around appreciatively. There was no doubt someone had taste and he assumed it to be Mrs Montfield. Indeed, she was elegantly dressed as well. All good, expensive clothes but no top designer labels which cost thousands. Her hair was that elegant subtle blonde and immaculately coiffed, making Paul wonder if she'd taken time out from the family crisis to have her hair done.

On her finger was the ring that Charlotte Chase had described. Could she have seen it somehow, on some other occasion? Sarah Montfield didn't appear in public very often and any photos Paul had seen were not detailed enough to show the ring. Samantha must have told her about it.

He shook his head, silently admonishing himself. He'd told Charlotte he believed in her and here he was doubting her.

"Please, Sergeant," Sarah said. "Sit down. Can I get you anything? Coffee, perhaps?"

"Thank you, but no."

He sat in a large wing backed armchair which may well have been the most comfortable chair he had ever sat in, and pulled out a notebook.

"Just a few questions," he said. "The body of a woman has been discovered. The body of Miranda Davies, the girl your daughter's fiancé is presumed to have run off with."

He couldn't fail to notice that Sarah Montfield gasped and quickly covered her mouth to suppress the sound. Was she really so squeamish that the idea of a corpse frightened her? Or did she know something about it?

"Mrs Montfield? You have something to say?"

She shook her head, clasped her hands in her lap and seemed to be arranging her features in a passive expression.

"Of course not, Sergeant," she said. "It was just the idea of one so young losing her life like that."

"Like what?"

"Really, Sergeant," Jason said quickly. "It is obvious if you have found a body as you say, and that you are here asking questions, that it was not a natural death. After everything this woman put my daughter through, of course my wife is distraught."

"Of course," Paul said quietly.

"So," Sarah said, "you think Simon did it? His note said he had left with her. Perhaps he didn't want to share the money after all."

"It is one avenue," Paul said. "But when I told your daughter about the discovery, she didn't seem all that surprised."

Jason slammed the mug he'd been holding down on the table, causing hot coffee to splash all over the polished surface.

"I've heard enough of your insinuations, young man," he said. "First you hint my wife might know something about this unfortunate young woman, then you accuse my daughter. I think it's time you left."

Paul did as he was bid. He had no real authority to stay once the owner of the house had requested that he leave and as he climbed into his car, he looked up to see Jason Montfield standing on his doorstep. There was no sign of his wife.

Miranda's body showed signs that she had suffered a frenzied attack. It could mean that Simon Chandler had lost his temper over something, beaten then strangled her. Perhaps it was something to do with their plan, perhaps something had gone very wrong and he blamed her.

He couldn't simply accept Charlotte's word that the letter hadn't been written by Simon, much as he would like to. He had never met the young man in question, but he had come from nothing, no family, no support to owning and running his own business. That earned Paul's respect, but he couldn't let that cloud his judgement.

Even without knowing him, he liked him a hell of a lot better than Jason Montfield.

CHAPTER EIGHT

Charlotte shivered as they entered the building and she opened her bag as she walked reluctantly to the ticket office.

"I suppose we'll have to pay," she said.

She handed over the price of two tickets to the clerk and collected a brochure containing a diagram of the parts where tourists were permitted to explore.

She allowed her eyes to skim over the brochure laying out the opening times, price of entry and all the other tourist things, then she gave a short laugh.

"God Almighty!" She exclaimed. "They charge people to stay here all night!" She tapped the glossy paper with the back of her hand. "Can you imagine that? If they could see what I see, they'd never set foot inside the place, much less stay the night."

"What do you see?"

Charlotte eyed her thoughtfully for a few minutes. Did she want to answer that? She wasn't sure she wanted the residents of this place to hear her. She shook her head but made no reply.

The corridors were dark, the stone walls were grey and there was a chill in the air from the lack of sunlight.

Men and women had been imprisoned here for years, starved and forgotten, and not just adults either.

At the end of the corridor Charlotte saw a child, a little girl no more than five years old. She wore a filthy dress that hung off her skinny frame and black shadows encircled her sunken eyes. She looked about to cry, but was trying to hold back those tears, probably knowing they would do her no good.

"Never mind," Charlotte said at last. "Let's get this over with."

"If Simon is here," Samantha said. "How are we going to find him?"

Charlotte looked back to where the child had now vanished, to be replaced by the wispy, transparent figure of Miranda Davies.

"Just follow me," Charlotte said.

She followed the spirit to a barrier rope which hung across a passageway with a sign hanging off it. *No Admittance - Staff Only.* She looked around to be sure there were no staff members to stop her then stepped over the rope, Samantha following close behind.

She placed her hand in Charlotte's and clasped it tightly, her heart beginning to pound so hard she was sure someone would hear it and come and order them out of this part of the prison.

The corridor disappeared into the dark as they moved farther along, the grey stone damp here and emitting a stench of staleness, like stagnant water. Charlotte wished she'd thought to bring a torch.

On both sides there were doors, old wooden doors with barred openings at the top, the only light the inmates of these cells ever saw. There were no windows on the outside walls, just more grey stone.

Their footsteps echoed on the stone floor as they walked, but Charlotte didn't notice. There were other sounds here to drown out that one.

Miranda had gone. They made their way warily along the narrow corridor, a slight wave of claustrophobia coming over Charlotte. And all the time, she could hear the cries of people trapped here, locked away in these cells for crimes they may or may not have committed.

She was never afraid of the ghosts she saw. Always they were either just carrying on the only way they knew how or they wanted something specific from her. But the spirits here were different. This was the place where they all had one thing in common; it was the place where they had spent the worst days of their lives, probably the last days of their lives, and they were trapped, just as they had been trapped in life.

And these spirits were malevolent. Fritz and Freya would never have come through here, even if Charlotte could have sneaked them in. They would have recognised the evil surrounding these phantoms and they would have fled.

Charlotte never visited any of England's ancient buildings where its violent past was best left forgotten. She had seen the same evil in many places as she saw here and it always left her wishing she could be an ordinary tourist.

She tried to ignore the ragged and skeletal figures who gripped the bars on the cells they passed, tried to keep her eyes firmly locked in front of her. She couldn't help them; if there was a chance she could she would have tried, but she couldn't. She had tried before, in other places, and it never worked. These phantoms were trapped here for a reason and she had only a suspicion of what that reason might be.

They kept walking, deeper and deeper into the darkest depths of the ancient prison. There was nowhere else to go except along this corridor, which got gradually narrower and thankfully became just lined with stones and dirt. The cells were behind them now, and there was no other sound.

"If Simon is down here," Samantha said in a trembling voice. "Surely he would cry out."

"Miranda has gone now, but she led us here."

"And ghosts cannot lie?"

"They can, yes, but not this soon after death. She has a conscience about you, about Simon, and I believe it is because she knows where he is and possibly played a part in his abduction. She cannot move on until she tells someone and that someone has to be me. No one else can hear her."

Charlotte was beginning to wonder if her confident words to Samantha were true. She had no idea where they had come from or how she knew the truth of them, and the further they went into the darkness of this awful place, the more doubtful she became.

And she was concerned for the dogs. She'd parked them close to the building and left the windows wide open, but she never left them this long and never where she couldn't see them. She couldn't stay here much longer, no matter how certain she was that this was the right place.

But what else could she do? She could hardly bring the police down here on the word of a phantom. She could just imagine the reaction she would get, no matter how much that sexy sergeant declared his belief in her.

"Is that another door?" Samantha said.

Charlotte breathed a sigh of relief. Right at the end of the corridor was another iron studded wooden door with a barred window. There was a light behind this one, a faint, flickering light as though it was coming from an oil lamp.

Both women picked up their pace and reached the door together, both standing on tip toe to peer through the rusty, iron bars. Yes, it was an oil lamp, and it stood on a small table beside a low, metal bed with a thin mattress.

Lying on the bed was Simon and he appeared to be fast asleep.

The door wasn't locked, much to Charlotte's surprise, and opened easily.

"Simon!" Samantha called to him.

She rushed to the bed and sank down on the floor beside it, stroked his face with her hand, leaned forward to kiss him. But there was no sign of awareness from him.

"He's been drugged," she said.

Charlotte pulled her mobile phone out of her pocket but there was no signal.

"Stay here with him," Charlotte said. "I'll get help. I wonder how they managed to get him down here without being seen."

"Hurry."

"I'll be as quick as I can."

She had to go all the way outside before her phone came alive and when it did, there were several text messages from Sergeant Middleton. She didn't have time to read those right now; he would have to wait.

The first thing she did was go to her vehicle to be sure her dogs were okay. They were fast asleep but both looked up when they saw her and came to the window to lick her face.

"Thank God," she murmured, hugging them. She kissed each one then turned back to the phone to dial the emergency services.

While she waited, she got the dogs out of the vehicle. She noticed a tap beside the massive front gates and turned it on for them to drink, then she put them back in the people carrier, and began to read the messages from Paul Middleton.

She noticed several people smiling and pointing at the dogs where they poked their huge heads out of the open window. She was used to that; everybody remarked on them wherever they went.

But the messages from Paul drew her immediate attention. Where was she? That was his first question and where was Samantha? Had they made any progress in finding Simon?

The pathologist had completed his post mortem on Miranda and it had been confirmed that she had been beaten and strangled. Charlotte could have told them that, but she carried on reading.

They were looking for Simon on suspicion of the murder of Miranda Davies.

CHAPTER NINE

She waited until the ambulance had arrived and loaded the unconscious Simon onto a stretcher and safely into the back of the ambulance before she rang Sergeant Middleton. She'd seen enough police programmes to know that when they believed themselves right, they'd go to any lengths to prove it.

Samantha tried to wake Simon, but he seemed to be deep in some sort of coma and they could only hope he wasn't injured.

The prison staff were shocked to find the paramedics following Charlotte to a part of the building that was never opened to the public. They were mostly volunteers who came to show the tourists around; there was only one permanently employed here: the curator, a woman of middle years with hair that was once auburn, but now fading as auburn hair tended to in later years.

"You can't go down there," the curator woman called out. "It's dangerous. The roof's not stable; that's why we don't let the public in."

"Well, you let someone in," Charlotte told her angrily. "Not only did you let them in, but you let them bring a kidnap victim inside and hide him there."

"Never!" The curator argued, shaking her

head vigorously.

"How much was the donation? I can imagine he made a generous one if you let him and his small group of special friends visit those parts that were closed off."

The Curator was still shaking her head, but the colour had drained from her face and Charlotte knew that she had taken a massive bribe to turn a blind eye. That was probably where the quarter of a million in cash had gone, since it was pretty clear now that Simon hadn't got it.

"Expect a visit from the police," Charlotte told her. "They might even want to charge you as an accessory."

Samantha rode in the ambulance with Simon. She looked up from stroking his forehead as the paramedic was closing the door and smiled at Charlotte, who climbed into the people carrier and gave the dogs a quick kiss before she drove home. She would phone Paul when she got there, once she knew Simon was safely installed in a private hospital ward, which she felt sure Samantha would insist on.

As she drove away, she glanced out of the driver's window and saw Miranda's form, almost transparent now and gradually fading to nothing.

***

At home she fed the dogs and put the kettle on. If ever she needed a pot of strong tea it was now.

She sat at the table and picked up her phone, called up Paul Middleton's number and waited for him to answer.

"Where the hell have you been?" He demanded at once. "I've been worried sick."

"Oh, why's that?"

"Why? Because you and Miss Montfield are treating Simon Chandler as a victim, when it seems more than likely he took the money then decided he wanted it to himself. Perhaps Miranda argued with him, perhaps that's why he beat her up before he strangled her. Either way, when we find him, he's going down."

"If he ever regains consciousness."

"What?"

"You asked where I was," she said. "I was doing your job, Sergeant, finding Simon Chandler."

"You found him? Where is he? I hope you and your friend weren't stupid enough to approach him."

"If we hadn't, you'd probably find another body in a ditch, only this one wouldn't be so easy to identify."

"I don't understand."

"Obviously." She paused and sighed impatiently. "We found him in the bowels of Porthgowan Gaol, unconscious. He'd obviously been drugged, heavily drugged. He's at Porthgowan Hospital. I will meet you there."

"There's no need."

"Yes, there is. Someone needs to be there for Samantha and it's not going to be either of her useless parents."

She loaded the dogs into the people carrier and drove back toward Porthgowan. She was weary now and were it not for the police and their insistence that Simon was a murderer, she could put her feet up in front of the television. Alas, that was not to be.

Still the journey wasn't long. She would have gone there straight from the Gaol but the dogs needed feeding and she was hoping she might not be needed again today. But Samantha was in no state to stand up for herself and her father had far too much influence for his own good.

She parked in the shadiest part of the car park, opened the windows and left the vehicle. It didn't take long to find the private room where Simon was still unconscious, where Samantha was still sitting beside him, tears running down her face as she stroked his forehead.

In his arm was a needle at the end of an IV tube, pumping some sort of fluid into his comatose body.

She turned as Charlotte entered, then glanced toward the corner of the room where Sergeant Middleton sat watching his suspect.

"How is he?" Charlotte asked.

"He still hasn't woken up. They can't give him anything because they don't know what he's taken and without that, they might not be able to do anything."

Charlotte turned to Paul.

"Well?" She said. "Do you now believe me?"

"I do, but whether my superiors will agree is another matter."

Charlotte looked back down the corridor.

"I expected a bigger police presence than just you," she said.

Paul's mouth twisted thoughtfully as though he wasn't sure whether he should give a truthful answer.

"I haven't told anyone," he said at last. "And that's between us three."

"I thought you were sure Simon was guilty."

"Guilty people don't usually end up drugged and hidden away in a place where no one is ever likely to find them. But I want to be here when he wakes up."

"When?" Samantha said miserably.

Simon stirred, mumbled something incomprehensible and his eyes flickered open. He looked up at Samantha and forced a smile through his cracked lips, squeezed the hand that rested in his, then closed his eyes again.

***

"What I want to know," said Paul, "is how

did you find him?"

The doctor had left, having assured them that the patient would recover and Paul was itching to know how this outcome came about.

"We had help," Charlotte replied after a moment.

"Help from who?"

"Remember you said you believed in me."

"Miranda?"

Charlotte nodded.

"I knew she'd passed over long before you showed up with the news. She led us to Porthgowan and without her we'd never have found him. Now we have to wait for him to regain consciousness and tell us who put him there."

"Water, please," came a husky voice from the bed.

Samantha was up and pouring from the jug beside the bed into one of those little cups with a spout, which she held against his mouth while he drank.

She put the cup back on the bedside table and leaned over to kiss Simon's cheek. Her lips moved to his mouth and gave him a long, loving kiss which Charlotte didn't think she had ever had from Peter, only when sex was to follow.

Perhaps that's why he thought it was something separate from love.

"It was my father, wasn't it?" Samantha said

as she sat up and took Simon's hand in hers.

She'd suspected it all along, but she was persuaded that she was kidding herself, that it was Simon who had extorted the money and run off with his ex-girlfriend. Still, in the back of her mind she suspected Jason; he was so used to everyone jumping to attention and doing his bidding. She couldn't believe him capable of murder though.

She was convinced Mandy's death was an accident, perhaps whoever he'd hired for this had got carried away.

Memories of her childhood were coming back to her as she sat here, memories of a loving father who always found time for his little girl, despite the hours he spent building his business. He bought her the best of everything, gave her the best education and even seemed to accept Simon, once he had turned down his attempted bribes and signed the pre-nuptial agreement.

She couldn't believe he would have done this, not really. How could he have kept up the pretence, he who was so forthright, who always said precisely what he thought? But there was no other explanation.

She turned to Paul.

"Does he know?" She asked. "My father, I mean. Does he know we've found Simon?"

Paul shook his head.

"No. I haven't told anyone yet, but I'll have to soon. I'd like to hear what he has to say first, if you're up to it, Simon."

"You can tell him," Samantha said.

Simon squeezed her hand again, pushed himself up while she hurried to plump up the pillows behind him so he could sit up. He turned to her, brought her hand to his lips and kissed it.

"It was my father, wasn't it?"

"No, darling," he said. "It wasn't."

Simon knew his statement was going to shock Samantha and hurt her deeply, but there was no other way. He loved her; he'd never wanted Jason's money but he never blamed him for suspecting him. He supposed if he was a rich man he would feel the same about a mechanic from a care home who came courting his daughter.

"What day is it?" He asked. "How long have I been missing?"

"A week."

"A week? And the wedding?"

"Never mind that now," Samantha said. "Tell me what happened."

He reached out for more water, which she held to his lips, then he leaned back on the pillows.

"It was the night before the wedding," he began. "I had just got my bag packed and my things together, tried on my suit and thought about how stupid I'd look in a top hat and tails."

"You'd look gorgeous. I told you that."

"So you say. Anyway, there was a knock at

the door and I heard footsteps running down the fire escape. You know with those iron steps, no one can escape without my hearing them. I never thought anything of it, thought it was just another congratulations card. I'd bought tickets for us to go to Paris and I was putting them into a card. I wanted it to be just right, so I didn't bother to open the door straight away."

Samantha remembered the fancy envelope that contained the letter she had thought was from Simon. Charlotte had been right, of course; the envelope was meant to match something quite different.

"You shouldn't have done that," she said.

"I wanted to," he answered. "I wanted one thing that wasn't paid for by Jason Montfield."

She kissed him again, held his hand so tight it almost hurt. She was so pleased to have him back.

"But you'd written my name on the envelope," she said.

He gave Samantha a puzzled look and smiled.

"How did you know that?" He asked. "Did you find the tickets? Can we get a refund on them?"

"I expect so."

Of course they hadn't found the tickets, or the card. Those things would have made it clear that Simon had intended to go through with the wedding.

"Anyway," he went on. "When I did get

round to opening the door, there was a parcel on the doorstep, stuffed full of cash. I didn't stop to count it, but it was a lot."

"Two hundred and fifty thousand pounds," Samantha murmured.

Simon whistled quietly.

"As much as that? Well, I brought it inside, naturally. Couldn't leave that sort of money sitting on the doorstep all night. It was about seven so I thought I might as well get it over with straight away. I phone your house to tell your father I was coming over with his latest offering to give it back."

"I knew it!" Samantha cried out. "I knew you wouldn't have taken his filthy money!"

"Did you, love? That means more to me and all the money in the world."

"What did he say when he answered the phone?"

"That's just it," Simon answered. "It was your mother who answered the phone and it was your mother who arranged the meeting."

"Mum?"

She looked at Charlotte as if for confirmation, but she looked just as puzzled as Samantha felt.

"I'm sorry, sweetheart. It was your mother who met me. She asked for us to meet at the beach house; said she didn't want anyone to see."

The beach house was the Montfield's private little house on their own private part of the beach. It was only accessible when the tide was right out. Jason thought it a great idea when he first bought the place, but nobody really used it much anymore. They were all afraid of getting trapped by the tide and having to climb up the rocks behind to get out.

"The beach house? Nobody ever goes there."

"I think that was the point. I'm such an idiot; I didn't question it. I just thought she was trying to be discreet, didn't want anyone to see us with all that cash. I don't know what I was thinking really. I just wanted to get rid of the money as fast as possible."

"What happened?"

"I'd put the parcel into a plastic carrier bag because it was easier to carry like that. I got to the beach house, saw the door was open and your mother was waiting inside, so I went in."

"Then what?"

"I heard voices as I got to the door. I thought it was your parents, but when I heard what she was saying, I tried to turn back. That's the last thing I remember until I woke up here a few minutes ago."

Tears began to spill over onto Samantha's cheeks as she thought about her gentle mother, the only one who had been on her side in all this. What was it she had said after the first row with her father. *I understand, darling. I know what it is to be in love.*

And all the time she was the one who was

plotting to buy Simon off, to frighten him away. She wondered if it was also her mother who had sent the thugs in to frighten him, except that hadn't worked either.

Samantha was distraught. How could she? How could her mother have made such a fuss of her, telling her she understood, pretending to be on her side?

"And my father? Did he show his face in all this?"

"Sweetheart, I don't even think he knew. Oh, he knew about the money, of course he did, but I don't think he knew about the abduction. From the way she was talking, I think she chose the beach house to avoid him."

His mind went back to that beach house, to the words he'd heard that made him try to escape at the last minute. He remembered her voice, talking to someone.

"Jason mustn't know about this," she had said. "He's gone soft. He's decided to let her get on with it, decided to give in. He thinks because Simple Simon won't be bought off he must really love her. As if that mattered. I won't have it. I didn't spend my life building up this business just to give it away to a bloody mechanic!"

***

Sarah Montfield was frantically throwing whatever she could grab into her suitcase when her husband appeared in the doorway. He stood for a few minutes, frowning, curious about what she was doing or where she was planning on going.

"The police are finally sending a chief inspector," he said. "What are you doing?"

"I'm getting out of here," she said. "You can entertain the chief inspector; I'm going before Simple Simon wakes up."

"Simon? They've found him?"

She tossed a local newspaper at him and he caught it against his chest. On the front page was a photograph of Porthgowan Gaol, an ambulance outside and paramedics pushing out a trolley carrying an unconscious main.

The headline read, in blazing letters:

KIDNAP VICTIM DISCOVERED IN OLD PRISON BUILDING.

Jason's eyes skimmed the article then he looked up at his wife.

"I don't understand, Sarah. The police will want to question us. You know I never approved of Simon, but who the hell would do this?"

She stopped what she was doing and stared at him, her eyes full of doubt.

"You really don't know do you? You go along, pretending you're the one who made the money, you're the genius behind the company."

"It's what you wanted, remember? I would have been happier for everyone to know the truth."

"The truth? You don't know the truth. You think I made our millions out of electronic cigarettes for addicts?"

Jason didn't answer for a moment. Of course that's how she made the money; she recognised the need at the very beginning of the 'let's give up smoking' phase and she jumped at it. She wanted him to take the credit because she said that even today, people would take more notice of a man. She was probably right and with his working class roots, people saw inspiration for their own ambitions.

Sarah had come from a more middle class background, had been brought up with a comfortable lifestyle if not a rich one and her father had lost it all. That's where her determination came from.

But what was she talking about now?

"Sarah, I don't understand you."

"You never did, Jason. My plan was to see Samantha married to someone of her own class, then move abroad somewhere. But that damned mechanic got in the way."

"I don't want to go abroad."

"I wasn't planning on asking you."

"Sarah!"

That's when the doorbell rang.

"Don't answer it," she said.

She squashed the lid of the suitcase down and fastened it, picked it up by its handle and made for the patio doors behind her bedroom.

"Sarah, what are you saying? You had something to do with Simon's disappearance?"

"Someone had to do something; you weren't going to. What I don't understand is how they found him. I thought I'd found the perfect hiding place; nobody ever went down to those cell in the basement. I paid that curator a small fortune to let me take a 'small party of friends' down there, just for a short visit. She was happy to take the money."

"You can't be saying you killed that poor girl."

"If she hadn't got in the way, she'd still be alive. She just had to follow him, didn't she? But she came in handy when it came to writing the note. Told me just what to say that Samantha might believe."

She realised she'd said far too much when a man's voice answered her question. He had slid open the patio door quietly, while she was venting her rage on her husband, and now he stood staring at her, waving his warrant card.

"You have our local celebrity to thank for that," he said.

EPILOGUE

At last, Charlotte could put her feet up in front of the log burner, now merrily burning away and warming her toes. The lamps were on in the sitting room of the old building, making the place cosy, and the baby bears were lying at her feet, their chins on their huge front paws, their eyes closed as they dreamed their doggie dreams.

All the ghosts were quiet. Miranda had gone on her way, having made amends for her actions in life by saving the life of the man she tormented. Samantha was still at the hospital; she'd refused to leave Simon's side, wanted to nurse him herself, and her father had arranged for him to be transferred to a private hospital where she could sleep in his room with him.

Charlotte wondered how long it would be before they could trust each other again, but it seemed Jason was a good man after all. He wanted to pay for an expensive honeymoon for the couple when Simon recovered, but he insisted they use the tickets he'd saved up for, the second class holiday to Paris.

Now that was settled, Charlotte hoped to settle down to her new life in this beautiful part of the world, to see what the future might hold.

THE END

Thank you for Reading …. I hope you have enjoyed this story and if you have, please consider my other books.

<u>*The Charlotte Chase Mysteries*</u>

The Missing Bridegroom
Bring My Baby Home

<u>*Ye Olde Antique Shoppe*</u> *– A time slip series*

The Edward V Coin
The Anne Boleyn Necklace
The Ripper Rings
The Roman Bracelet
The Confederate Cap
The Tarot Cards and the Rosary
The Miniature and the Swastika
The Egyptian Headdress
Letter from the Tudor Court
Hitler's Notebook

<u>*Historical fiction/romance*</u>*:*

The Romany Princess
The Wronged Wife
To Catch a Demon
The Gorston Widow
The Crusader's Widow
The Minstrel's Lady (winner of the 2017 e-festival of words Best Romance)
The Adulteress

Conquest
A Man in Mourning
The Cavalier's Pact
Shed No Tears
The Outcasts
The Secret of Ainsley Gate
Daughters of Trengowan
The Million Dollar Bride

<u>*Factual:*</u>
The Loves of the Lionheart
For the Love of Anne

<u>*Series:*</u>

Holy Poison – a six book series telling of the ordinary people who lived through the brutal reign of Bloody Mary

The Judas Pledge
The Flawed Mistress
The Viscount's Birthright
Betrayal
The Heretics
Consequences

Summerville – Sequel to Holy Poison

Pestilence – A three book series set around the Black Death

The Second Wife
The Scent of Roses
Once Loved (winner of the 2018 e-festival of words Best Historical Novel)

The Elizabethans – A three book series following the lives of three noble brothers and what they sacrificed for love

The Earl's Jealousy
The Viscount's Divorce
Lord John's Folly

<u>Knight's Acre</u>

Book One – Till Death Do Us Part
Book Two – The Forgotten Witness
Book Three – The Countess of Harrisford

The Hartleighs of Somersham – a Regency tale

A Match of Honour (winner of the e-festival of words 2018 best Historical Romance)
Lady Penelope's Frenchman

<u>Other Books</u>:

Old Fashioned Values
The Surrogate Bride (a historical fantasy)

Mirielle
The Longest Shadow

<u>Short Stories</u>:

Taking Care of Mother
The Gatecrasher

If you would like to receive notification of future publications, as well as special offers, please sign up to my newsletter here Or visit my website http://www.margaretbrazearbooks.com

Made in the USA
Las Vegas, NV
05 February 2025